This Is Not the Tropics

Library of American Fiction

The University of Wisconsin Press Fiction Series

This Is Not the Tropics

Stories

Ladette Randolph

The University of Wisconsin Press
Terrace Books

The University of Wisconsin Press
1930 Monroe Street
Madison, Wisconsin 53711

www.wisc.edu/wisconsinpress/

3 Henrietta Street
London WC2E 8LU, England

1   3   5   4   2

Printed in the United States of America

Library of Congress Cataloging-in-Publication Data
This is not the tropics / Ladette Randolph.
p.   cm.
ISBN: 0-299-21510-5 (cloth: alk. paper)
1. United States—Social life and customs—Fiction.
I. Title.
PS3618.A644 T48   2005
813'.6—dc22   2005005452

Terrace Books, a division of the University of Wisconsin Press,
takes its name from the Memorial Union Terrace, located at
the University of Wisconsin–Madison. Since its inception in 1907,
the Wisconsin Union has provided a venue for students, faculty, staff,
and alumni to debate art, music, politics, and the issues of the day.
It is a place where theater, music, drama, dance, outdoor activities, and
major speakers are made available to the campus and the community.
To learn more about the Union, visit www.union.wisc.edu.

For my children
LEIF, JORDAN, and BRONWYN

Contents

Acknowledgments

Previous versions of these stories appeared in the following publications:

Prairie Schooner: "The Girls"

Passages North: "A Member of the Family"

Blue Mesa Review: "It's Cheaper to Live in the Dark"

South Dakota Review: "Billy"

Clackamas Literary Review: "What She Knows"

The Writers' Forum: "The Sensitive Man"

Karamu: "Dill"

The Heartlands Today: "The Blue Room"

This collection has had the benefit of feedback from many who read it in earlier versions. Thanks to Alison Rold, Judith Slater, Hilda Raz, Gerry Shapiro, Marly Swick, members of the No Guilt Writers Guild: Liz Ahl, Chauna Craig, Charlotte Hogg, Kate Flaherty, Sandi Yannone, Gay Gavin, Sherrie Flick, as well as my good writing partner, Erin Flanagan. And thanks always, for everything, my husband Noel.

This Is Not the Tropics

What She Knows

pizza boy

The pizza jiggles wantonly in the box the delivery boy holds open, a marketing gimmick, she guesses, some shenanigan Romeo's has trained him to do, holding the box open so the pizza can be inspected.

"I didn't order a pizza," Annie says.

"Oh." The boy looks down at the pizza.

"I wouldn't order Romeo's."

The boy looks up at her over the opened lid of the cardboard box. Their eyes meet and though he does not smile she feels a sudden weakness in her knees.

"You didn't order the pizza?"

"I didn't order the pizza."

"Okay," he says, but he does not move to leave right away and Annie makes no gesture to usher him out.

She wishes suddenly she were older, forty perhaps, the sort of woman who could say to the boy, "You could come in, though. You could stay for awhile. I'll

3

get you something to drink." She wouldn't be specific about what she would get. She hasn't imagined that far.

And though the delivery boy wouldn't say anything, he would be interested. She would go on then. "You need to leave the pizza outside, though. It's making me sick." She wouldn't tell him she was three months pregnant, and that the smell of grease from the melted cheese, and pepperoni, and sausage had created a nauseating ruckus in her stomach.

He is gone now, but before he left she noticed his shiny reddish hair had been slicked close to his head, his smooth cheeks recently shaved, though she could see he did not need a razor very often. He had smelled of aftershave. A certain moist quality on his skin suggested he had bathed only recently, that he had taken care to be well groomed.

She regrets she will not be the one to lead him into experience, will not be the memory he smiles upon when he is no longer the pizza boy but the man responsible now and wishing for newness and first times and innocence.

work

All day, at any given moment, an insipid song can be heard simpering through the PA system—"Close to You," "Cracklin' Rosie," "Muskrat Love." It is aural terrorism. The office Annie shares with another woman is small—a storage closet the company converted into a

4

space for two computers and a shared printer, shelves above small desks. All day long insurance salesmen come to her office with letters barely legible, badly written, full of outrageous misspellings and ask Annie to type them. She does so, automatically making the necessary changes. At the desk behind her the other secretary, very young, clacks away on the keys of her computer. She sniffles all day. Allergies. Annie brings her bee pollen and sinus/allergy tablets. The other secretary, her name is Janey, thinks Annie is so nice. Actually, Annie can't abide the sniffles. It makes her sick to think of other people's snot.

Jimmy Dare is one of the insurance salesmen. This is his real name. Annie suspects his parents found it in a comic book. In his spare time he trains dogs; he drives a '67 Ford pickup with striped seat covers coated with dog hairs. He owns two coon hounds. When he arrives for work in the morning his suits are slightly rumpled and often covered with dog hair. Annie tells him to dust himself off, if she notices, when he is leaving for a sales call. Jimmy Dare is the worst speller of all the salesmen. His dogs are named Doug and Joe. Annie thinks these are stupid names. Dogs should be named something like Baxter or Winston or Taffy so people know it's your dogs and not your friends you're talking about.

Jimmy doesn't talk very much; he's the least talkative of the salesmen, but when he gets started about dogs he can go on forever. Annie knows more than she wants to about the mating, and eating, and hunting habits of coon hounds. Jimmy reads everything he can get his hands on about them, and Annie thinks he's smart in spite of not being able to spell. One day he got started in her office about how Doug is such a great stud his services are in demand all across the country.

"People pay big money for stud services. I've shipped Doug from Pennsylvania to Louisiana to do his duty."

"How much does it pay?"

"Five hundred dollars plus expenses."

"Expenses?"

"Board, fees to and from the airport, you know."

Jimmy gets excited talking about these things. His eyes shine and he tugs at his hair, clutches it in his fists. It's a little weird but not entirely without appeal. He looks like a little boy then.

"You'd be surprised how many people want a good coon hound to stud."

"Yes, I would be," Annie says.

"Dogs are a lot like people," he says. He says this all the time. Everything a dog does is a lot like a person.

Annie went out with Jimmy one time. He took her to see an action movie— *Terminator 2*. She didn't like the film, but she liked having Jimmy's arm around her shoulder. Afterward they went for pizza. It was like a high school date, comforting and familiar and boring. He didn't ask to come in but she invited him. He seemed a little bewildered by the invitation.

"I've got a beer in the fridge," she had said. Jimmy livened up.

"Okay."

Once he was in the apartment he kept talking about dogs even as she kissed him on the back of the neck. It didn't take long though, it was pretty sudden in fact, for him to respond with a slight snorting groan, like a bull. Afterward, he had to leave right away.

"The dogs'll wonder where I am."

She hadn't planned on using Jimmy Dare for stud services. At one time she'd wondered what it'd be like to have a baby, and for a little while when she was with her last boyfriend she'd thought about trying to get pregnant. But when they split up she was glad it hadn't happened. Now, she isn't sure what she'll do. One thing she knows for sure, though. She isn't going to tell Jimmy. He doesn't need to know. Men are a lot like dogs, she thinks. She doesn't want to be in this position, doesn't know what she's going to do. When she sees Jimmy Dare in the office after their date he acts like nothing ever happened between them. She doesn't even think he remembers. That's okay. It wasn't all that memorable anyway.

families

The problem with families is that they want to get together on every holiday, especially if they're within driving distance. Easter is the holiday Annie hates most. One Easter her mother made her hide eggs for the kids early in the morning. The grass was wet, and the wind was blowing, and it was raining. Later, even the little kids hated hunting for eggs in the rain. Her mother never learns though. This year it's Memorial Day.

They've planned a picnic. Late in May, a picnic is in order, only when the morning arrives it's that same rainy thing again, except not a warm rain like you would expect in May; it's freezing cold. Annie can see her breath on the air. It's Monday morning and she wants to be sleeping in. Her mother wants to hear the Legion Club band play taps at the cemetery. Annie doesn't even bother to ask why this is meaningful. She stops by the deli and buys a quart of potato salad to contribute to the picnic. In the rain, she drives to her parents' house.

"Good morning," her mother says cheerfully. "Are you ready to go?"

There's nothing wrong with her mother really. She's a nice woman as far as mothers go, but for some reason the entire family gets on Annie's nerves. She's the only one who isn't married and doesn't have kids. Only her father seems to understand. He doesn't say anything. That's just it. He doesn't speak. It's his way of protecting himself. He stays out of the way and as soon as he can, he sneaks off to the garage or the backyard or the basement, somewhere where the little kids won't find him.

Annie's oldest sister complains about her father's disinterest in the grandchildren. "I don't understand Daddy. He shows no interest in the kids." She says this at every family get together.

This morning Annie and her father exchange a glance. Outside it is pouring rain, but her mother goes on humming as she packs a picnic basket.

"Aren't you a little worried about this weather, Mom? It's not exactly picnic weather."

"We have a lot of time for the weather to clear up. It'll be nice this afternoon. You just wait and see. Gene, can you get me the folding table from the basement?"

Her father goes to the basement. "Can't we just assume there will be picnic tables where we're going?" Annie asks.

"We could, but I don't know anything about this park. There may be a lot of people and then we wouldn't have a table."

That's how things go with her. She's an optimist with no reason for optimism. The day never does warm up and all the kids are rotten—sick and cranky, with chapped, red faces—and Annie can still see her breath on the air. Plus, she's got morning sickness.

"You look a little green around the gills," her mother says.

"I'm okay."

"Are you eating right?"

"I'm eating fine."

"I know how you young girls eat—Doritos and M&Ms—just junk. You fill up on junk and then there isn't room for nutritious food."

"Let her be," Annie's dad finally says. "She's an adult."

"Thank you," Annie says.

After lunch, which has taken place under a shelter in the middle of the empty park, where all the plates have blown away, and everyone is shivering in their coats, stamping their feet, the kids decide they want to put on a play. They've been rehearsing it while the adults were still eating. Now, as their parents tell them there won't be a performance, they're angry. They're shouting at the adults, carrying on. Annie never wants to have kids. In light of this day, she never wants to have kids. She feels a little square of panic, like a field, and it's growing. She simply can't do it. No kids.

an appointment

The doctor's office is too bright. He has posters on the ceiling with chimpanzees in various silly costumes, and captions that anthropomorphize an expression the chimp wears. They're meant to make you smile while your legs are spread and your butt is hanging off the edge of the table and some strange guy wearing rubber gloves has his hand up you. Annie isn't smiling. She's grimacing as he removes the speculum.

"You're right. You're a little over three months along." He takes off his gloves and writes something in her chart before turning to her. "You can sit up now."

Annie struggles to sit up. The doctor doesn't seem to notice her trouble. When she's finally sitting up he looks at her. "It's late, you know."

"Yes."

"It's not easy at this point. There aren't as many options."

"Yes."

"But you still want to go ahead?"

"I have to."

"Why do you say that?"

"Because I do."

"That isn't really an answer. Does the father know?"

"I don't know the father," she lies. "He wouldn't care anyway. I'm just another bitch."

The doctor frowns. "Do you care to explain that?"

"No."

"I'm concerned about this. I'm not sure you've thought it through."

He's been her doctor all of her life, and he's tapping the pencil now, looking at the chart. Doctors never seem to understand that not everyone wants their opinion. Her life has nothing to do with what this doctor thinks.

"You're twenty-two years old?" He looks up.

"Yes." Annie isn't sure what he wants her to say, what he's looking for.

"Are you absolutely sure you want to go through with this?"

"No."

"Then I think you need some more time. I'd like to see you try to track the father down. It's not fair to him not to know."

"Why is it a problem that I'm not absolutely certain?" she says. "I won't be absolutely certain I want it either. Why is that uncertainty okay and this isn't?"

friends

Annie's favorite bar is The Dude. She goes there to dance. Even though it's a gay bar they welcome everyone—lots of straight people go there to dance because the dancing is in a group, not just couples. Annie thinks it's very generous of The Dude to allow straights to come since there are so few places for gays to be by themselves.

The bands are usually good, hardcore. She likes to mosh. Tonight she thinks the moshing may be a good thing. She drives into the group, her head lowered, her elbows raised, and starts pushing and jabbing and jumping. This feeling of being pushed along in a group of sweating strangers is hard to describe. She doesn't expect people who haven't done it to understand how fun it is to feel slightly threatened, exhausted, full of energy and rage. Rage is good. She feels a lot of rage and this is the only place where she can express it. She screams and no one hears, not really, because they're screaming too.

A stocky guy with short, bleached hair elbows her, hits her hard, slamming against her upper arm and shoulder. He knocks her into another guy who knocks her back. She laughs, meeting their hits with her own. But then the blond guy's elbow slips, catches her in the stomach, and knocks the wind out of her so she doubles over. This is not a good position to be in when bodies are flying around. The guy is nice, though, and pushes her to the edge of the pit so she can recover without getting her head stomped in.

She sits at a table on the side panting, trying to catch her breath. That's exactly what she wanted, a good sharp jab in the stomach. She feels satisfied to watch the others dance. While she is watching, her friend Dana walks in. Dana is wearing a purple miniskirt with multicolored, horizontal-striped tights and a midriff T-shirt that shows off her flat stomach and her delicate bellybutton. Dana has the best bellybutton of anyone Annie knows. Dana knows it too.

"Why're you sitting out?"

"I got socked in the gut."

"Oh."

"You going in?"

"Later." Dana opens her bag. "I've got treats."

"I don't think I want any."

"Suit yourself," Dana says and leaves the table for awhile. When she comes back she is smiling, her eyes glassy. She giggles when she sits down beside Annie. "So what're you thinking, my main girl?"

"I'm not thinking much of anything."

"Good for you."

They watch as the swirling, slamming bodies surge to the music. On the stage the lead guitarist drops to one knee and plays a solo. Annie thinks he's a wanker, a double moron. This is not her favorite band—the Ma-tilda Quotient. Dana doesn't agree. Dana thinks the lead guitar player is a babe. She sighs now as he plays his solo. He looks down at her. Dana follows this band, and they're used to having her in the audience.

"You're such a groupie, Dana," Annie says now.

"He's in love with me. Can't you tell?"

Annie looks back to the stage. Although the guitar player is looking at Dana, he doesn't seem to see her. "He's in love with himself."

Dana is disgusted and lights a cigarette. "You're just jealous he's hot for me."

"Whatever. Give me one of those." Annie reaches for the pack of cigarettes hanging halfway out of Dana's black bag. She leans forward to accept a light from the tip of Dana's cigarette. After taking a deep drag she leans back. "Whatever you say."

the morning after

In the morning Annie is disappointed that nothing has happened. She slept through the night, waking up with a slight headache, her clothes smelling strongly of smoke, a rancid, left-over smell. She hates the smell of smoke from the night before and decides to go to the park to get out of the house. She doesn't know what she thought would happen, but she imagined that it might have been like this: She might have gone home, sat on the toilet, and gotten some heavy cramps, a little stronger than she gets during her period, and then she might have felt something slip between her legs, something a little thicker than a clot. She might have flushed the toilet without looking and then gone back to bed. In the morning everything would have been okay again.

At the park a little boy who can barely walk plays in the water at the edge of a fountain. He keeps trying to crawl into the water and his mother has to pull him back. This makes him laugh. For a while he is content to trail his hand in the water, but soon he's trying to crawl in again. His mother is patient, and though she scolds, she doesn't get cranky. Finally, she says, "Since you don't want to listen to Mommy we'll have to play somewhere else."

The baby begins to cry. Annie is surprised that he is able to understand what his mother has said. She has noticed he only speaks a few words and not in complete sentences. Children are smarter than she imagined. A child could be smarter than she is. This is not a comforting thought. There are so many reasons why she wants to stand on a relatively tall building and jump, a building not so tall that she will die or necessarily even get hurt very badly, but a building tall enough to break the life growing in her. She doesn't want to be responsible for a life like that, and yet she can't seem to bring herself to stop it. She hadn't imagined she'd be so wishy-washy about something like this.

While she is at the park she thinks about telling Jimmy Dare about the baby. She wonders what he would do. This is what she knows he would not do: He would not sweep her into his arms and call her darling. He would not tell her he wants to marry her and take care of her and the baby. He would not clean up his house, and get rid of those coon hounds, and invite her and the baby to live there. He would not paint the baby's room pale yellow and put white curtains at the windows. He would not smile lovingly at her by a fire in the evening.

After that Annie thinks about what she would do if she were to keep the baby and raise her, because she knows already it will be a girl. This is what she would do: She would wake up early and feed the baby mashed bananas and Cheerios. She would point to the squirrels out the window playing in the trees, and then push the baby in a stroller around the block. When they came home she would make a grilled cheese sandwich chopped up into little pieces for the baby. She would read to her from little books and make animal sounds for each animal in the alphabet book. And at night she would rock the baby to sleep under a soft blue blanket embroidered with illustrations from nursery rhymes.

thrifting

On the best days she feels as though someone died and she went to heaven. On those days there are dresses, and hats, and purses, and rhinestone jewelry from someone's estate, vintage things she finds before the specialty shops find them and mark up the prices. On those days she drags home sacks heavy with treasures. She washes and mends the clothes, reglues the rhinestones. The hats and purses she likes and has good intentions of using but never does. She sometimes goes through her things and plans to give them away, but then she invites Dana over to take what she wants first. Only Dana always stops her.

"You could wear this to a barbecue," she says holding up a sleeveless gingham dress with a matching short jacket. Or, about a black, off-the-shoulder dress, "Don't give this away, it would be perfect for going to the opera." And later, in regard to a full-skirted appliqué dress, "You can't pass this on, you could wear it to a dance at the Pla-Mor." Annie doesn't have the heart to give away anything once Dana has stopped her, although she is amused by the social life Dana has fabricated for her. "A barbecue? The opera? A dance at the Pla-Mor?"

Dana shrugs. "You never know."

Today, as Annie is looking through the racks, before she realizes it she is looking for dresses a few sizes too big, for smocks or other long tops, for pants with elastic waists. Once she sees what she's doing she goes to the maternity section. A vintage outfit—sleeveless pink crepe, a top and skirt, very Jackie O. She pictures white gloves and white shoes, a pillbox hat. Perfect for Easter Sunday. Easter Sunday? Lord. The suit is inexpensive and she buys it.

When she tried the suit on in the thrift store, it fit perfectly across her hips and flat stomach. Later, at home, she puts the suit on again. This time she takes a pillow from the bed and stuffs it under the skirt, adjusting the ties at the waist to accommodate this new girth. Once she has pulled the top over she admires her new self in the mirror, turns from side to side inspecting herself. Not bad.

Maybe tomorrow she will go back and see if there are any baby clothes. She deliberately avoided them this time. She might check to see if there is a crib or high chair, something in a nice '60s blonde wood finish. Retro baby. She imagines little bell bottom pants and a corduroy jacket, a small necklace of beads she will make. Then she catches herself. What is wrong with her anyway? She wouldn't have guessed it would be like this. Everything in her life had seemed simple in theory.

research

The library downtown is old. The marble steps inside are listing slightly to the west. There is a stale smell of old carpet and books, but Annie doesn't mind the smell. She goes to the electronic card catalogue most remote from the entryway just in case someone she knows should come in. "Babies" she types as the subject category. Up flash hundreds of listings with subcategories like Discipline, Toilet Training, Nutrition, Day Care, Fathering, even things that strike her as strange like The Family Bed, Massage for Baby, Your Baby's Past Lives. After looking through several of the titles she feels discouraged. Among the titles she has seen in the card catalogue is *Your Baby and Downs Syndrome.* After that, she feels dizzy and nauseated; the panic has returned. I can't do this, she thinks.

She goes to the section where the books are shelved anyway. Once there, Annie finds several old editions of baby care books, titles from the 1950s and '60s. She flips through the pages seeing photographs of mothers with infants, the mothers all so outdated they've become cool again. The babies look just like babies always do, only now she looks at them more keenly, sees that they differ in big ways. They aren't all just the little, plump, bald-headed things she's imagined them to be. The books make her feel uncomfortable though. There seems to be so much she doesn't know—bathing, diapering, feeding, breast-feeding, burping after meals. Everything requires more thought and effort than she expected. Where would she find the time?

Annie leaves the library without any books. Her head is spinning a little as she walks back out into traffic. Although she is in a crowd walking toward the bus stop, she feels very alone, isolated, as though she is invisible. No one seems to notice her, and she hugs the knowledge of what is happening to her to herself. She doesn't want Dana to know or her mother and sisters. All of the people who might be of help to her she fears will also be a danger.

This is what will happen if she tells her mother and sisters: They will be angry at first because she isn't married, but then they will become protective. They will make plans, take her under their wing, force her to move out of her apartment and into someplace closer to them. They will give her boxes of hand-me-down baby clothes and hand-me-down maternity clothes, paint and furnish the nursery the way they like it. She won't need these baby books because they'll all tell her what to do, give her endless advice and not realize they're contradicting each other. The whole thing will take on a life of its own, an energy and scope far beyond anything she has yet understood about being a woman in the world. And it won't stop there, she can see how she will be appropriated into the stream of life around her, so far avoided or ignored—schools, doctors, clean air, crime. She begins to see how she will be afraid, vulnerable in ways she has not imagined.

Annie's bus comes, charges to the curb, stands huffing and snorting, and then roars away without her. She hasn't had the heart to get on and sit in cramped seats so close to strangers. The air seems too hot, a mixture of diesel and the perfume of people she doesn't know.

a visit

Doug and Joe bound about Annie. She can tell they want to jump on her but are too well behaved.

"Doug, Joe. Stay back," Jimmy says now in a gruff

voice, firm and yet affectionate. The dogs grow subdued, though they still pant and grin at her.

"Will they let me pet them?"

"Sure," Jimmy says, "but you'll have to put up with a little licking. It's how they get to know you."

Annie reaches out tentatively, her hand high above their heads, and touches both dogs with just her fingertips. The dogs slather her with great wet tongues, thick as Turkish terry cloth.

"Nice doggies," she says even though she is totally grossed out by their tongues. She is trying to understand Jimmy's life. This is a mission she's on, trying to get to know Jimmy. The dogs do not lose interest as she had hoped they would. They continue to circle her.

"Back guys," Jimmy says. He shoos them from the door and invites her in.

His house is what she expects, cluttery and none too clean, stacks of magazines—mostly dog training journals, but a few sports magazines as well. There is an antique girlie calendar above the sink with a slightly chubby blonde woman in a kittenish pose. Among his things are other signs of his taste in Americana, a few Pyrex and Fire King bowls in the sink, a black panther lamp, a yellow enamel kitchen table and vinyl covered chairs. He doesn't invite her to sit down, but she sits in one of the kitchen chairs anyway.

"You want a beer?" he asks.

"No thanks."

"You mind if I do?"

"Go ahead."

He isn't curious as to why she doesn't join him in a beer, doesn't know her well enough to know that this is an exception, that she's sworn off it temporarily without really admitting it to herself until now. He doesn't offer her anything else but sits down in the chair beside her, tipping his beer back in a big swig before setting it down between them. When he looks at Annie she feels suddenly shy, silly. Why has she come here? What did she expect to happen? Did she expect him to see her and know? No, she's not that dumb, it's something else, something to do with loneliness and with needing to be with someone even if they can't really help. Jimmy is a little weird in this way, and she knows it from their first encounter. He doesn't assume the way other men do; he has to be led along, prodded, primed before he'll act. It's an unusualness she sort of likes, but right now she feels frustrated as he looks at her again before taking another drink. He's questioning, too, what she wants, senses, she can tell, she isn't here just passing the time.

Annie lacks the urge and the energy to seduce Jimmy tonight, though she has to admit that's what she wanted. She can't seem to muster the stuff of seduction, the smiles, the lowered lashes, the brushing of limbs, the stories. It is not about sex, this longing she has, it's about belonging somewhere with someone. Somehow the stranger who has taken up residence makes her feel more alone than before. But this isn't going to work, this fix she's hoping for from Jimmy.

"I just stopped by to see the dogs," she says. "They're nice dogs."

"Thanks." He doesn't seem surprised by this. She realizes that though he may not be stupid, he is thick in some way. He's sort of sweet, but she can't depend on him.

As she leaves, the dogs circle her again, licking freely this time, and Jimmy doesn't tell them to stay down. She can hear them howling as she drives away, sees in the rearview mirror their heads thrown back baying at the sky. Crying? Saying goodbye? She doesn't know.

sunday afternoons

Okay, she admits it, she gets depressed on Sunday afternoons. Something to do with going to work the next day, feeling washed out from the night before. Dana comes over this Sunday, as she does most Sundays so they can hang out together. They listen to music, or shove sections of the newspaper to each other, or watch old movies on TV. Dana yawns a lot and says she's bored and dreams about things they could do. "We could go over to the art gallery, see the exhibit there, Egyptian jewelry."

Annie grunts, "Yeah."

A few minutes later, "We could go to the Children's Zoo. That would be kind of a kick looking at the animals and watching the kids."

Annie does not reply. Dana scrolls through a list of

potential sites of amusement, many of which require some amount of planning like advance tickets, all of which require energy that neither of them seems to have. This futile dreaming, a combination of boredom and wishful thinking, depresses Annie worse than before. She feels suddenly very impatient with Dana.

"You don't seem interested in doing anything. Is something wrong?" Dana asks.

"It's just that we aren't going to do anything anyway, and I don't feel like the obligatory 'that'd be nice.'"

Dana looks pained. "We might do something."

"We might, but we won't, so why talk about it? I don't have the energy."

"You've been talking about not having any energy lately. What's the matter with you?"

Annie is quiet. She doesn't know how to respond to this, has forgotten how to make the small talk that would throw Dana off track. She doesn't mean to, but tears squeeze through all of her reserves. She can see Dana is upset, moving now to hold her, which is the last thing she wants, someone being nice to her. It will only make it harder, but Dana is there with her arms around her shoulders, rubbing and jostling in that way meant to cheer up the person who has momentarily lost control.

"Don't be nice to me, Dana. It makes me feel worse."

"I know, but I don't know what else to do. I can't just sit here and watch you cry."

Annie has to laugh a little, wiping her nose with the back of her hand.

"You want to tell me what's going on?"

"Not really."

"Listen, I noticed something seemed to be wrong the other night at The Dude. I think you need to talk about it."

"There's not much to say."

"It doesn't look like that."

Annie thinks for awhile. She thinks, this is what Dana will not do: She will not leave her alone. She will not resist buying baby clothes and little books. She will not be quiet about it and let her figure things out on her own. She will not sit demurely listening as Annie tells her how she feels and what she's considering. She will not let her believe that she still has options. She will force her to realize that the time for options has passed. She will not be silent.

Dana is looking at her strangely. "You look pale. Are you feeling all right? You look a little sick."

"I'm not sick."

"So . . ." Dana gestures for Annie to go on. "Tell me what's up."

"I'm pregnant."

Dana laughs. "No way. No way."

"Yes way."

"Oh Jesus. I'm sorry to laugh, but that's so funny, Annie."

"I don't think it's funny. Why do you think it's funny?"

"I can't say. It's just making me laugh. You as a mother. Wow. What are you going to do?"

"I don't know."

Dana grows quiet. "Pretty heavy stuff, girl. How long have you known?"

"Oh, a couple months."

"A couple months? And you didn't tell me?"

"I didn't tell anyone."

"Who's the father?"

"Some dork."

Dana nods. "Wow. So what are you going to do?"

"Don't keep asking me that. I don't know."

"How far along?"

"Four months."

Dana raises her eyebrows. "I guess I don't need to tell you . . ."

"You don't need to tell me."

milk

Dana is at the door. She's holding a gallon of milk. "For you," she says as Annie opens the door. "You need to be taking care of yourself. It's not enough just to stop doing stuff that's shitty for you, you have to start doing stuff that's healthy."

Annie feels exasperated. She wishes she'd never told Dana.

Dana walks through the apartment. She seems purposeful, looking at the ceilings and the walls.

"What are you doing?"

"I'm figuring out some way we can make a nursery

in here. The way I see it, this room could be divided, put a divider here, see." She steps back and paces out the area she is talking about. "You could get a simple divider and then the baby would have some place separate."

"Dana, this is making me tired, talking about all of this. Why are you assuming things?"

"But I have to. And you're probably feeling tired because you aren't eating right. Let's get a glass of milk down you now."

"God, I never figured you for a nurturer. You'd think it was you having this baby."

Dana shrugs.

"What does that mean?" Annie mimics the shrug. "Just because I'm pregnant doesn't mean I'm an invalid. It doesn't give you the right to come in here and tell me what to do, and what to eat, and where to put things. It doesn't give you the right to turn my whole life upside down. I wish I hadn't told you. I knew this would happen." Annie doesn't mean to but she starts to cry again.

"See, you're all worked up. I'm not trying to be bossy, but Annie, it's pretty clear, you're not dealing with this thing. I bet you haven't even told your folks yet, have you?"

Annie shakes her head.

"Well, that's okay, but you still need to get real here about what's happening. If you don't want to keep the baby your options are getting narrower all the time. It's past the point, you know, for getting rid of it easily. It'll be harder, and if you want to give it up you need to be making contact with an agency." Dana reaches into her big black bag. "Here, I've brought you some stuff. A prenatal book so you'll know what's happening and some brochures from adoption agencies. It's still an option to abort but it'll cost you."

"Jesus." Annie plunks onto the couch.

Dana lays the materials on the coffee table. "I don't mean to overwhelm you. I'm trying to help."

"You're not."

"You think that now. Later you'll thank me."

"You sound just like my mother. "

Dana laughs. She picks up the gallon of milk she's set on the floor and carries it into the kitchen. Annie hears her open a cupboard. From the kitchen she yells, "There's a free clinic downtown where you can get a check-up without it costing you an arm and a leg. There's also a program, government assistance you know, to help you if you decide to keep the baby and still work."

Annie sighs deeply. She tries to avoid looking at the book and brochures on the coffee table, but notices one title. "'Seven Sorrows of Our Sorrowful Mother Infant Home'?" she reads aloud. "Are you trying to drive me over the edge?"

"Sorry about that," Dana shouts from the kitchen. "I was in a hurry."

The cover of the prenatal book, featuring a plump, smiling baby and a serene, beautiful mother, has seared its way into her corneas, and Annie keeps seeing it even though she isn't looking.

"Here," Dana says and thrusts a large glass of milk into her hands. "Drink it."

Annie looks at the size of the glass. "I can't just sit here and drink a whole glass of milk like this."

"Of course you can. You have to. I'll distract you."

"I don't see how milk is going to make everything all right, Dana."

"It won't, but it's a gesture, a good faith gesture to your body."

resignation

The computer guys have come to fix computers at work. It is not only Annie's computer but a string of computers apparently spooled together that have malfunctioned. Because her computer is down, she cannot do the work she had planned and spends a lot of time looking at the walls and the shelves and Janey's back as she, whose computer is not down, works diligently, just like one of those little clerks described by Victorian writers, toiling away, their backs rounding to the work. Annie cannot believe she works in this place, has worked here for three years. The lack of a computer screen has afforded her this broadened view of what she does and where she spends hours of her day.

Jimmy Dare stops by. He meets her squarely in the eye. This unnerves her a bit, but she recognizes it as a habit of his, only she hadn't noticed before because she was always avoiding eye contact. He seems to look carefully at her.

"You look different," he says.

"Really? How?"

"I can't say, just different."

"I don't think so," she says. She's not about to get into any of that with him.

Before he leaves her office he says, "I hope they get your computer up pretty soon."

As he says this, she knows it isn't going to make any difference at all to her if they get her computer up. She's not coming back, not tomorrow, not the next day, and not any day after that. She's going to walk out of this rat hole tonight and never look back. She's going to do something irresponsible, and risky, and rude, and she isn't going to worry about it. Already she knows this, that she isn't going to worry about it. Jimmy Dare is only part of the reason for her leaving. It's true, she doesn't want him to see her change. His scrutiny is too much, and she doesn't want to deal with what will happen when she can no longer lie so easily and get away with it. But it's much more than that. It's the fact that she feels like she's going to die if she keeps sitting here in this closet that isn't a closet anymore simply because some executive sitting on his fat ass in a big airy office has said, "it's not a closet anymore, it's an office now."

She spends the afternoon taking her things from the drawers in her desk and putting them into an empty computer paper box. She does this surreptitiously, the box between her feet, so that even Janey doesn't notice anything until the end of the day when she picks up the box to leave and Janey says, "What's in the box?"

"I'm just taking a few things home."

No one else mentions the box, and Annie carries it through the lobby. She looks around briefly one last time and smiles to think about what will happen the next day, what people will think. The one thing she knows is that no one will think what is true. While she was waiting to leave at the end of the day, she doodled for a while and then she wrote, This is What is True:

Truth #1: This place sucks.

Truth #2: These people are too white, all of them, so white their eyelashes are white.

Truth #3: People shouldn't have to work in closets and call them offices.

Truth #4: I shouldn't have to see Jimmy Dare every day.

Truth #5: I'm going to have this baby and I don't want to listen to their talk.

groceries

It's a good time to find a new job. No one is allowed to ask if she is pregnant and she doesn't yet really look pregnant. In the job interviews, the few she has, if some interviewer asks slyly what her future plans are, hoping of course she'll say something about a family, she is especially careful. *No future plans particularly.*

31

There aren't any good jobs out there right now, so she interviews for boring, dumb jobs like working in a department store selling shoes, clerking at Kmart, daytime clerking at Gas & Go, working as a tech at the regional center. A good job might be working in a coffee house or a record store. The job she ends up taking is at the B&R grocery store on Washington Street. First thing, they give her a dark blue smock with her name embroidered on the left where there would be a pocket if there was a pocket. The smock has long sleeves, and buttons up the front. She hates blue.

Every week she has to memorize a list of the prices for produce and the specials for the week. She goes home on Wednesday nights and memorizes: rutabaga—79 cents a pound; cilantro—two bunches for a dollar; Japanese eggplant—$1.99 per pound. This doesn't mean she would necessarily recognize this produce if it came through her register. The first week she tried to figure things out, asking the customers what the weird produce was, but she got tired of doing that pretty fast and started making up things. Now if it looks like an apple, it is an apple. If it looks like a cucumber, it is one. Someone only stopped her once, but they were stupid. The thing they were buying cost $1.00 more a pound than the thing she had credited them with.

It's been a month since she started this job. Things are getting easier and the manager is a strange-but-nice guy who likes her. No one has noticed anything yet because her smock is roomy and because when she comes to work she never crosses her arms across her stomach. She likes the freedom and flexibility. The pay ends up being about the same as her old job.

She'll tell them soon about the baby, once they've gotten to know her better. She has a feeling they'll understand. She has a feeling they won't mind at all what she does. Strange things happen here all the time. Her news will be nothing compared to the drunk who took off all of his clothes in the store a few nights ago, or the stabbing in aisle nine the week after she arrived. The manager tells her this sort of stuff happens all the time. What could one little baby matter to them?

a vision

"And this is the sorting room where our volunteers sort the maternity clothes and baby clothes we get from the lovely people who pass them on to us," the woman from the clinic is saying as they walk by a large room with a linoleum floor and fluorescent lights where women stand among deep piles of clothing. "Once the clothes are sorted, they're cleaned and hung here for our mothers to choose from." She gestures to racks of clean clothes. All of the clothes that Annie sees look like Lutheran clothes, very bland—belted dresses in pastels or pale floral patterns, slacks with permanent creases, and button down short-sleeved shirts. Lots of blue, and gray, and turquoise. The baby clothes are equally boring.

"Should you need babysitting in a pinch," the woman is saying, "we've got a clinic day care for temporary situations." Today as they walk by that room only four or five children are playing with an older woman. "We can take up to fifteen children at a time, more in case of a real emergency. And we will take a sick child should you need it." Annie exchanges a quick look with Dana, who has come along with her. Dana smiles. Annie is happy to know about these things. The woman has already given her a list of possible day care providers and their addresses and phone numbers so she can drive by and look at the houses before calling. All of the workers and volunteers at the clinic are women. They smile a lot and wear their hair straight and natural. Annie likes them, though she doesn't feel entirely comfortable with them. They're all a little too nice. But she feels better knowing about this place, and they've been giving her monthly checkups all along. Today she is getting a tour of postnatal support.

Things in the building are a little rundown: the design in the linoleum floors are worn thin; the walls are scuffed, though clean; the ceilings are fake wafer board, with tiles broken here and there. The fluorescent lights flicker now and then. It's depressing as hell, but Annie can't afford to get depressed about things like this.

Several weeks ago, she sat her parents down to talk. They both seemed nervous about her formality and even her mother couldn't quite find a way to make things smooth and easy. Annie stuttered around a bit, but then she looked at her dad and he smiled at her. She wanted to cry when he did that.

"Okay," she said and took a deep breath. "This is the thing. I'm just going to say it straight out. I'm pregnant. I'm about six months along," she said, ignoring her mother's gasp. She glanced quickly at her father. His face did not change expression but his eyes still met hers. "I haven't just been gaining weight."

"Well, I . . ." her mother started.

Her father nodded. Neither of them said anything for a long time. Annie sat across from them with her hands folded together on the table and willed herself to be serene, and to wait until they were ready to talk. When they were ready, did they ever talk. Her mother mostly. She answered few of their questions in a straightforward way, but she talked enough to make them feel their concerns were being addressed. She'd rehearsed her answers for the big stuff like, what was she going to do now? She had prepared enough so that even though that energy and life-of-its-own she had feared threatened to take over, she wouldn't let it. She rode that impulse from her parents like she would have a cart with a slightly wild horse at the reins, and she wouldn't let them have their head, just let them go the distance until they settled down by themselves.

When their conversation was over she was proud of herself. She had held onto her version of how things would go and they hadn't talked her out of anything. Maybe she'd be okay with this baby thing after all.

Since then her mother has been respectful. Annie must have made it clear that she didn't want them to meddle and that if they did they simply wouldn't be welcome in her life. Her mother seems humbled, smaller somehow. She calls ahead before coming over and always asks politely before assuming Annie wants something from her. Given that climate, Annie is more receptive to her mother's advice or gifts.

Her sisters were a little more difficult to manage, not as easily subdued as her parents, big in their bossiness. They took a lot of license to tell her what to do and what not to do, and how dumb she had been, but they were easy to ignore.

Now, at eight months along, everything is growing strange for her, like looking simultaneously through the wrong end and the right end of a telescope: the people around her seem very small as they move about soundlessly, scurrying to where she doesn't know and doesn't care; and then looming before her, herself: her big belly, her swollen feet, her every twitch and cramp. And at night, dreams so vivid she feels as though she has to swim up from a deep pool every morning to wake up. This is what she knows now from the dreams: The baby is not a girl, it's a boy. He will have red hair the color of carrots, which she will cut short in spite of the cowlicks that will stand up at the back of his head like twin fans. Freckles will cover his sharp little nose and sharp little chin. He will wear glasses and be very thin, very petite. He will play the trombone in the grade school band, playing with gusto at home as he practices, showing off for her how he can make the trombone sound like an elephant, and playing timidly in the band concerts at school where his teachers will tell her he is a quiet boy, a little shy, with few friends. But he will be a genius in math, an early reader, and he will dream of playing someday in the NBA, reading eagerly the sports section of the daily newspaper, filling her in on the statistics that week of his favorite players. He will walk with one foot slightly turned in, his shoulder blades narrow and sharp through his short-sleeved, striped jersey shirts, his elbows jutting out and his arms, in those same short sleeved shirts, freckled like his nose. And she will love him. And he will break her heart, not by being any sort of disappointment or trouble, but simply by being hers.

A Member of the Family

Lena Bradfield walked past her mother three times at the bus station before she recognized her. It was her hair. Dyed jet black, it had been ratted and back-combed into an elaborate bouffant.

"Ma?" Lena said when she finally recognized her. "What'd you do to your hair?" Her mother seemed bewildered by this greeting and absently patted her hair as though to remind herself what had happened.

"It looks like Elizabeth Taylor's," she said then.

"Says who?"

"Myra, over at Geltone."

"Don't believe it for a minute," Lena said.

Her mother's face fell. "It doesn't look like Elizabeth Taylor?"

"It looks like shit, Ma," Lena said, then swooped to kiss her and help her to her feet. She picked up her mother's suitcase and the paper shopping bag she always brought filled with newspapers, knitting, half-eaten packages of cookies, and canned foods. Her mother clutched a bulging black patent leather purse.

"How are you?" Lena asked as they pushed out the door of the bus depot.

"Oh, you know."

"How was the trip out?"

"Long. I talked to a nice lady who got on in Pennsylvania. She got off in Iowa. She was going to visit her daughter too. We don't understand what you're doing all the way out here in the Midwest."

Lena opened the trunk and loaded her mother's things. "Ma, why do you bring so much? You think we don't have newspapers or food in Lincoln?" Her mother shrugged and smiled vacantly.

Once everything had been packed in the trunk, Lena helped her mother into the passenger side of the car.

"Where's Carl?" Her mother looked around the car as though she thought he might be hiding in the backseat.

"He's at home. You'll see him when we get there."

Carl made dinner that evening, his specialty, Thai Lemongrass Soup. While Lena cleaned the dishes afterward he asked, "Mrs. D., would you like a bump of scotch?"

"I'd like that," her mother said. They took their glasses into the living room. Once she had finished in the kitchen, Lena joined her mother and Carl.

"Carl's just told me about the news—Rocko's estate," her mother said, eyes sparkling with the effect of the scotch.

"I told you about that when I picked you up this morning," Lena said irritably.

Her mother looked away. "Oh, that's right. Sure you did."

Carl shot a scolding look at Lena. She liked that, him scolding her.

"So Rocko's dead then?" Lena's mother said. "Lorenzo didn't like him much."

"No," Lena said.

"$200,000 he's leaving?" her mother said. "Where do you think he got it?"

Lena raised her eyebrows. "It doesn't take a genius."

Her mother smiled. "No, it don't take a genius. Do you remember the story Lorenzo always told about him throwing the dog off the roof of the building?"

"No, I guess I don't," Lena said.

"That's funny. I thought he told that story all the time." Her mother shrugged. "And Lorenzo? What happened to Lorenzo?"

"Pop? You mean, Pop?" Lena looked startled.

"Yeah."

"Pops died, Ma. He died a long time ago. Remember?"

"Aw, sure I do. I remember now."

Carl cleared his throat. "What would you like to do while you're here, Mrs. D.? I only have one appointment early tomorrow morning, so I'll be free to spend some time with you."

This time it was Lena's turn to send a scolding look.

"That's nice of you, dear," Lena's mother said. "There's really nothing I want to do, just spend some time, play with the kids, I guess."

Carl coughed softly. "Yes. You remember, of course, the kids are gone. But I was thinking maybe we could go over to St. Theresa's tomorrow morning and play bingo."

"Yes, that'd be nice," Mrs. D. said. She yawned then. Her small body was plunked on the sofa like a stuffed doll, her feet dangling off the floor. Her face was pale and doughy.

"Your bed's made up, Ma," Lena said. "Why don't you go ahead and get some sleep."

"I think I will."

Once her mother had been settled, Lena came back into the living room where Carl was working on his second glass of scotch and reading the local piano tuners' guild newsletter, *The Action*. His long angular body was folded onto the couch. The lamplight reflected a little on his balding head, over which he combed a few longish strands of blond hair. He looked up as Lena entered the room.

"Just what do you think you're doing?" Lena hissed, "horning in on my mother's time here. I'd think you'd at least have the decency to be especially busy this week. The less she sees us together the better."

"I like your mother," Carl said.

"What's that have to do with it?"

"I want to spend time with her. I always do when she comes. She'd think it was odd if I didn't."

"I don't like it," Lena said. "You're taking advantage of her visit to make a point."

"And what point would that be, Lena?"

"Keep your voice down," Lena whispered hoarsely. "You know very well what you want. You want to keep everything the way it is, act like nothing has changed."

"How do you know what I want? I don't know myself what I want." Something in Carl's tone took Lena off guard. "I've got to get some sleep, Lena." He stood up. As he passed her, he hesitated then lightly touched her arm. "I'm tuning the Grantham's piano early tomorrow. I'll try not to wake you."

"Ma, let me wash your hair out for you," Lena said noticing the way her mother's new bouffant hairdo lay smashed against one side of her face when she woke up the next morning.

"If you want, dear," her mother said, patting her hair in the same distracted way she had the day before.

After breakfast Lena gently situated her mother's head under the faucet of the kitchen sink, where she directed the spray of warm water onto the artificially black hair.

"That feels so good, dear," her mother's muffled voice said.

Lena was gentle as she sudsed the hair, massaged the scalp, and then rinsed. After her mother's hair had been toweled off, combed free of tangles, and blown dry, Lena set to work with the electric curling iron. Her mother's white scalp looked stark and fragile in contrast to the black hair she parted and sectioned off.

"You're sure quiet this morning," Lena said as she scrutinized the curl she had just turned out. "You feeling okay? Did you sleep well last night?"

"I'm okay," her mother said. She seemed to be thinking about something.

"What's up, Ma?"

"That's what I want to know," her mother said.

Lena was surprised by the tone of voice, a commanding, confident tone Lena remembered from her distant childhood.

Lena suspended the curling iron for a split second then resumed her work. "What do you mean?"

"There's something wrong here."

"What are you talking about?"

"You and Carl. Something's wrong."

Lena suspended the curling iron again. She felt like a child caught lying. She did not answer her mother for a while as she wound another curl. "Okay, Ma," she said finally. "You're right." Her mother did not answer and Lena repeated, "You're right, Ma. There's something really wrong." Lena's face fell as she spoke.

Her mother turned sideways in the chair. "What's the matter, dear?"

Lena straightened her back, sucked in a deep breath, and made a show of wiping her tears as casually as she could. Her mother seemed curious rather than upset by the tears and stood up awkwardly to take the curling iron from Lena. She laid it on the kitchen table. "Let's go into the other room for a while," her mother said as she led Lena into the living room, where they sat together on the sofa. Her mother patted her back, "Ssh, ssh," she said. "It'll be okay. Everything'll be okay."

Lena allowed herself to be comforted. Edna, the cat, sensing something was wrong, insinuated herself between them, sharing their laps.

"What's the matter, Lena?" her mother asked again.

"It's nothing, Ma. I just needed a good cry." Lena stroked the cat's yellow fur. Edna purred loudly. Her mother was quiet. Lena said, "Have you ever felt like everything was the way you thought it was and then on a normal day, everything just the same as always, you brush your teeth, you shower, you dress, you drive to work the way you always do and then the worst thing happens, in the middle of all of that ordinary stuff? The worst thing happens when you don't expect it?" Lena glanced at her mother. She seemed not to be listening.

At Lena's glance, though, her mother roused herself. "Yes, I think I have," she said.

Lena noticed her mother's hair then, straight and limp on one side of her head and full of uncombed curls on the other. "Let's finish your hair, shall we?"

"Oh, sure," her mother said. Edna woke, stretched her back, and jumped to the floor.

On Saturday afternoon Carl and her mother left to play bingo at St. Theresa's.

"Good luck, Ma," Lena shouted. "Pay attention this time so you don't sit there with a bingo and not know it."

"That was just a little oversight, wasn't it, Mrs. D.?" Carl said as he helped Lena's mother over the door's threshold.

"What was that?" Lena heard her mother ask as they left.

In the mail later that afternoon Lena received a registered letter. It came in an ivory parchment envelope, its return address in an elegant font—Epstein-Goldman Agency. She held the letter for a while before sitting down to open it. Inside the letter officially laid out the terms of her inheritance—Rocko's estate, left to his brothers and sisters and their children, had been left unclaimed in the New York City courts for several years. By now, none of the brothers or sisters were left, only the nieces and nephews. There were eleven of them, their names listed in alphabetical order. There she was—Lena D'Amico (Bradfield)—fourth down, below her cousin Elizabeth and above her cousin Lennie (Leonard). She hadn't seen any of them for years. For one second a memory, playing on the streets in front of their buildings, someone's mother yelling from a window above, a community of children, playing with, protecting, and exploiting one another.

Her share would come to a little over $18,000, which, she figured, by the time the lawyers were done with it, would be considerably less. But still. A little money all her own. Not entangled with Carl in any way. $18,000. Not a fortune, but enough to help out. With what? With her own life should she and Carl decide to split? Should he decide to leave? She didn't like that scenario, her waiting on his decision, left in the house as he packed and went away, abandoned, passively sitting by and letting someone go. What did she want? It was she, she realized, not Carl, who wanted things to stay the same.

"I have a surprise for you, Ma, one of your favorites." Lena set the hot casserole dish on the table.

Her mother sniffed. "What is it?"

"One of the dishes you used to make all the time when we were kids, one of your favorites—lentils and macaroni."

Lena's mother frowned. "That? I never liked that."

"You never liked that?"

"I never liked that."

Lena sat down. "I just thought . . . we had it all the time . . ."

"Lorenzo liked it, it was one his mother cooked. It was all we could afford. I haven't made it in years."

While she spoke, Lena's mother served herself from the casserole. She took a large helping.

Lena shook her head slightly; Carl caught her eye and smiled. She returned the smile automatically then caught herself. They hadn't exchanged a smile in a month, not since she'd found the note in his jacket pocket. "So Freudian of you, Carl," she had told him. "Well, I don't want to be a participant in your little drama."

Carl had blushed. "I'm afraid you already are."

"Go to hell," she had said.

After her mother went to bed that evening, Lena knocked on the door of the bedroom she had shared with Carl. She had moved out the month before. From inside Carl called, "Come in." He seemed embarrassed as he motioned for Lena to sit down on the edge of the bed.

"It's my goddamn bedroom and I'm feeling shy," Lena said and remained standing.

"Me too."

Lena looked around. The room was different without her clothes hanging in the closet. The tall oak dresser was bare where her things had once been set out. Her own absence was palpable. "I like what you've done with the place. It gives new meaning to the spare in spare bedroom."

Carl motioned for her to sit down again. She sat on

the edge of the bed, away from Carl. She glanced at him quickly then down at her hands. "So what's he like?"

"Who?"

"You know." Lena looked up then and Carl flushed.

"Oh," he said.

"How old is he?"

"Lena."

"Just tell me."

Carl looked away. "He's 23."

Lena blew out a quick breath. "Younger than Ben and Lisa? My God, Carl." Carl did not respond. "Is this the first one, the first time you've . . . Is this the first time?"

"Yes," Carl said. He looked straight into her eyes. "That's the truth."

"How'd you meet him?"

"Lena, please. What are you wanting to accomplish?"

"I need to know."

"Paul Peterson," Carl finally said.

"Paul Peterson? Paul's introducing you to young men, I . . ."

"It's not what you think."

"Then what is it?"

"It was the apprentice thing. Remember Paul's neighbor who apprenticed with me last year?"

"That Jeff?" Lena's shoulders sagged. Her whole body felt weak. "Of course. I should have put it together. So how long . . . ?"

Carl's back stiffened. His eyes narrowed slightly. "What difference does it make?" he said.

"I have a right to know." Lena looked down at her hands again. They were large hands, too large she felt for her body. The skin was wrinkled and dry, the nails clean and clipped close. They were practical hands, working hands, she thought to herself. They were not hands equipped to understand complexities. They were hands that acted. Hands that found being in doing. Hands that scraped carrots and scrubbed toilets and paid bills and weeded flowerbeds and typed letters and rubbed backs and mended clothes and refinished furniture.

"What are you thinking, Lena?" Carl asked, gentle now.

"I'm thinking about my hands."

On Sunday morning Edna woke Lena early.

"You beast," Lena said. Edna nudged Lena's forehead and purred. Outside the sky looked like curdled milk, lumpy with clouds, a pale light on the horizon. Lena fed Edna and made a pot of coffee. Outside it had started to sprinkle and the wind gusted hard as she opened the door to pick up the morning paper. She was purposeful as she laid the newspaper across the table and immediately opened it to the section announcing "Apartments for Rent." She remembered then how her first waking thought had been a picture of herself and Edna in a sunny one-bedroom. It had been a cozy thought. As she ran a finger down the rental section, she began to decorate—in the kitchen a nice palm, not too big, and a small oak table with two chairs. Two chairs? Who would visit? The children? Coworkers? Suddenly, the coziness she had envisioned earlier became simultaneously very lonely and very cramped.

A momentary panic. She righted herself. Lately, her mother's visit, the news from Rocko, had taken her back to her childhood, to memories she thought she'd forgotten. She thought about the thread of her life, just her, not the unit of herself and Carl she had grown accustomed to through the past thirty-one years of their marriage. She found it exhilarating, both frightening and exciting, to remember she was a human being in her own right, independent of Carl. As a young woman she had always thought of herself in those terms, but after marrying Carl, she'd stopped. It had seemed selfish somehow.

From the hallway, Lena heard someone stirring and quickly found a new place in the newspaper. It was Carl.

"Coffee's made."

"Thanks."

This was how it was now between them—one of them stating the obvious, the other being grateful.

"Your mother leaves tomorrow." Carl poured a cup of coffee.

"Yes."

He sat down at the table and Lena folded the paper to make room.

Neither of them looked at the other. Her mother's arrival had forced them to make contact in a way that in the previous month they had avoided. They were speaking now and Lena sensed they both felt the obligation to make a decision, to leave this suspension of time, to act, if only to fall apart.

One more day. It was a countdown.

Later, her mother padded into the kitchen in the oversized pink slippers she had brought, a Christmas gift from Lena's sister, Dora.

"For the cold," her mother had told Lena that first night. "My feet never warm up." And Lena remembered that now. She set the teakettle on and found an old dish tub and a bag of Epsom salts in the bathroom closet.

"What's this?" her mother asked as Lena gathered the supplies.

"For your feet."

"My feet?" Her mother frowned. "What's wrong with my feet?"

"They're never warm. You said that. 'My feet are never warm.'"

"So?"

"I'm going to soak them and rub some of the blood back into them."

Her mother rested her elbow on the table and

cupped her face in her hand. She watched Lena skeptically without comment.

"I know," Lena said in response. She set the tub on the floor at her mother's feet. "For once don't fight me. Just go along."

Her mother shook off the too-big slippers and edged her blue-veined, yellow-nailed toes toward the water, tentative, toe tips first, she winced at the water's heat and pulled back.

"A little more cool?" Lena added cool water then helped her mother ease her feet into the water. Her mother groaned. The water slapped softly against the sides of the tub.

"What's all this about, this waiting on me?" her mother said.

"I don't know . . . your feet. You're not getting enough circulation."

Her mother rolled her eyes. She sighed then. "You remember your cousin Joanie?"

"Sure I remember Joanie." Lena glanced up quickly then continued to rub the sole of her mother's left foot.

Her mother nodded. "You remember she ran out in front of that car, didn't look? That was terrible."

"Of course that was terrible, Ma. What are you getting at?"

"You should know."

"Well, I don't know."

"We were poor, all of us. Everybody was working too hard. God knows I wasn't there, not really, nobody was really there," her mother said. "And Lorenzo keeping me up half the night yelling and throwing things, drinking himself stupid, night after night and me trying to get up and go to work at the cannery the next day." She frowned. "None of us could keep anything nice. It either got broken or Lorenzo pawned it." She nudged Lena on the shoulder. "Remember your cross from confirmation? Remember that?"

"I remember."

Her mother shook her head. "Aw, it's no good going back. No good going back. Somebody should have been there to watch Joanie, though. She was only two, crossing the street by herself. What were we thinking?"

"I don't know, Ma." Lena had stopped rubbing her mother's foot. "I really don't know."

"That's just it. You don't know. You just have to live and be stupid and suffer."

Lena laughed and set her mother's foot back into the water.

The next morning Lena and Carl took her mother to the bus station. The bus was delayed and they sat in the waiting area. Lena felt nervous and perched on the edge of the seat.

"Why do you bring all this stuff?" she said to her mother as she noted again all the bags and sacks. "Why not just bring a bedroll? You could camp out here while you wait." Her mother smiled. "Did you remember everything, Ma?" Lena said, feeling suddenly anxious

53

for her. Her mother nodded. "And you'll be sure to wait for Dora to pick you up when your bus gets in, right?"

When the bus finally came, Lena was relieved. She didn't want to be responsible for her mother any longer. Before she boarded the bus, her mother had hugged her tightly and whispered, "You take care, dear."

"I will," Lena said. "Don't let Myra get her hands on you, Ma. No more of that Elizabeth Taylor shit."

"Take care Mrs. D. We'll see you soon," Carl said as he bent to hug her.

The afternoon was bleak, the sky the color of cement. The winter ground was hard, mud gray, and dry. In the wind the trees rocked and groaned, their skeletal limbs raised as if in supplication to the cold sky. Trash scudded across the pavement and gathered against curbs.

In the car going home Lena and Carl were quiet.

"I hate days like this," Lena finally said. "I wish we were going somewhere."

"Where would you go?" Carl asked.

"Someplace green where the wind never blows."

Carl smiled. "Mexico City or Hawaii?"

"Mexico City hands down. You?"

"I'm with you. Mexico City."

Lena grew quiet. She looked out the window. "We've had a nice life."

"Yes," Carl said.

"And now everything is different, isn't it?"

Carl nodded. Lena laid her head against the car window. The glass felt cold against her skull. A greenish light sifted through the clouds as they drove past block after block of tiny houses on the southern edge of town. There were no children on the sidewalks, no elders on the front porches, no teenagers loafing and teasing on the streets. The dregs of winter. As she began to sink into depression, something in Lena's mind was quick to reroute her thoughts. Tomorrow was another day, it pointed out. Spring was just around the corner. Old things die and new things come to life. Her mind was like an obnoxious hall monitor. Whose side was it on anyway? She wanted to slap the voice to silence, felt impatient with her own internal insistence on self-hypnosis, wanted to face her reality square on. No use fooling herself. If only Carl hadn't—but no, it was no use placing blame either. Blame would get her nowhere and only end up destroying her and Carl and the children as well. No. She was determined they would do this with some sort of dignity. None of which changed the fact that the whole thing was enormously sad. Lena felt shaken to the bone as she thought about it. Chilled. Weak. Was this what people meant when they said they were devastated? But even in the midst of such feelings, she found the situation absurd. Laughable even. Laughter had always gotten her through the hard times before and she sensed the cusp of that laughter now. She felt that same laughter as she thought about Rocko's estate. Absurd.

She didn't know why she had lied to her mother. She remembered well the story of Rocko killing the dog. It had been the only story her father had told of his childhood, and Lena had always visualized it vividly. She always saw Rocko, looking like Marlon Brando in *On the Waterfront,* leaning against the door that led onto the roof of the tenement where the four brothers were living together. He was the oldest of the boys. That day they are all wearing T-shirts. It's a warm November afternoon. The sunshine is why they've taken the ball onto the roof, to play with the young German shepherd pup they found that spring. Though the pup has grown to almost her full size, she still has that puppy energy and awkwardness. Round and round she chases the ball as the young men tease and hoot, her tail wagging, tongue dangling, a silly dog grin on her face.

Then without warning Rocko stands up. He moves toward the dog and picks her up. Her body bucks and twists in his arms as he walks to the edge of the roof. She whimpers softly before he throws her over the edge. The others watch in disbelief. On the street below they hear the barely perceptible thud of the dog's body hitting the ground, a soft cry on impact and then silence. A crowd has gathered on the street below, all of them pointing up.

"Why'd you do that Rocko?" her father says. "Why'd you do it?" He is crying, unashamed of his tears which he does not wipe away.

Rocko takes the cigarette dangling at the corner of his mouth between his fingers and tosses it to the tar paper roof. He grinds it slowly under his black boot and then, still without a word, turns and walks away. Lena always pictures how his tight T-shirt stretches across the muscles of his shoulders, how a pack of cigarettes is wrapped in the sleeve. Her father starts after him, his fists balled tight. But Rocko hesitates slightly, tenses through the shoulders and her father backs away, afraid.

Later, the three younger boys go downstairs and onto the sidewalk where they pick up the dog and find a place to bury her.

But that was her father's story. That was how Lena had pictured it all the times he had told the story when she was a child. Today Lena pans across that familiar rooftop once more, and this time she notices how the dog sees Rocko out of the corner of her eye, glances quickly toward him and then away, distracted by the ball. When she is suddenly lifted into the air by his strong arms she is confused for a moment, desperate to right herself. The position in which she is being held is uncomfortable, but she isn't frightened, not yet. Even as she feels herself lifted higher she is not afraid, though she whimpers slightly, a question. And then there is a moment of suspension, nothing to support her, but still no fear. Only a great noise, a pressure as she falls and things run together. A whine escapes her throat, a small whine, so distant she can't hear it, it has nothing to do with her, does not relate to her. She is not thinking as she falls for the noise and the blur and the pressure. And then suddenly that last moment, the final thud and gasp, the involuntary bark, again so distant it can't be hers, and a strange coldness followed by a seeping warmth. Knowing it isn't really so bad as she turns inward away from the press of people, the faces above her as they close in. She is unaware of their stares, unaware of herself. Everything is lost. And she understands now, how there is nothing so worth keeping that its loss does not somehow set her free.

The Boy in the Band Uniform

The boy in the band uniform was standing in Samuel's kitchen when Zoe saw him from the hallway. Behind the boy she glimpsed through the garden-level window the sidewalk and the steps that had brought him into the house. She hadn't heard him come in. Samuel chopped an onion for the stew boiling on the stove. He did not acknowledge the boy's presence. Samuel was a surgeon, and she had seen him cut like this, precise and firm, during surgery at the field hospital where they had met. Zoe was a nurse. The boy stood stiff and still, at attention, but he did not seem ill at ease with Samuel's silence. Nothing indicated he had just spoken, though Zoe had heard him before she entered the room, "Sir, we have no food. We need food. Will you help?"

The band uniform had obviously been tailored to fit the boy's slender body. The thick fabric bunched slightly, but otherwise the tailoring was expert. The uniform had been carefully pressed as well. He wore also a white plastic hat with a chin strap. The white plastic had yellowed everywhere except for a white patch in the middle where an insignia of some sort had been removed.

In the other room Zoe heard Samuel's friends William and James laughing together. She understood finally they were mimicking the boy, marching and saluting, collapsing together in laughter. Grown men mocking a boy. This hilarity over the misfortunes of others still shocked her. No matter how she tried, she could not find a way to understand it. She had seen it numerous times, how people ran from their houses if they heard an explosion nearby, not with concern or even curiosity, which she might have understood, but with glee. Excitement. Tragedy an entertaining spectacle.

There was the day she had been traveling by jeep between hospitals when she and the driver had come upon the scene of a terrible accident. A large crowd had gathered, yet no one made an attempt to help. There had been no survivors. Although the bodies had not been disturbed, no one showed any sign of moving on. Instead, among the gawkers was a feeling of elation, hilarity even, as people took turns miming what had happened bringing the crowd to laughter, or striking the poses of the dead to great approval from the group. They were slaphappy over catastrophe. She justified the behavior by telling herself it was how they dealt with so much pain and suffering.

Still, the way William and James were carrying on

now made it hard to extend her theory to this situation. When she looked back to the kitchen the boy was gone. Samuel had finished chopping the onion and was now cubing the mutton. The smells were wonderful. Samuel did all the cooking. Each evening he came home from the hospital and cooked as a way to forget the day.

"Where did he go?"

Samuel did not look up from his work. "I sent him along."

"So quickly? What did you give him?"

He looked up at her then back down to his work. "I gave him nothing."

Zoe went to the window and looked out on the street. The boy was nowhere to be seen. "Nothing? Is he coming back?"

"No. I can't encourage this sort of thing. It will start a problem."

She knew she shouldn't ask, but she did, "What sort of problem?"

"You're letting your feelings get in the way again, Zoe." He was right. Her feelings were getting in the way. This was Samuel's house, his food. She couldn't offer what wasn't hers, but she could go out on the street and find that boy and give him what he needed or go with him to find it. She had admired the boy's initiative. Unlike so many others, he was not sitting on a street corner begging. She had been impressed with his desire to look smart and sharp, how he had taken it upon himself to go ask for help. Samuel was waiting when she spoke, "You haven't answered my question," she said. "That was an enterprising boy. He was a nice boy."

"I don't know anything about that boy except that he's part of a gang. His little charade is only evidence of their craftiness. People . . . foreigners," he said and looked at her significantly, "will fall for the trick. In a few weeks we'll be reading in the papers about the scam, how the kind patron was blackmailed or how their apartment was burglarized, and the foreigners will be irate."

"You can't know that."

"Can't I?"

"No. How could you? His mother, his grandmother must have helped him. The band uniform was tailored to fit."

In the other room William and James whooped at this. They appeared in the doorway then, leaned against one another. Medical students on break, they were dressed casually, their shirts untucked, their baggy pants creased. They would return to classes the following week where they would wear their white coats and stand straight. But for now, they slouched together with their arms around each other's shoulders. They said nothing to Zoe, but William saluted her. It was enough to send James into another spasm of laughter. Even Samuel smiled, though he did not meet her eye.

"What is the matter with all of you?"

Samuel added the mutton to the pot, sliding if off

the cutting board with the broad edge of the knife. He covered the pot and turned down the heat before slowly washing his long, graceful fingers under the tap. He dried them before turning back to her. Samuel was a kind man; she knew this about him. "Zoe," he said. "You must not assume that mothers and grandmothers cannot form a gang. Please do not assume these things." He said it as though he was concerned for her safety. Entreating rather than explaining.

She had been living in the capital city for a few weeks because the fighting had come too close to the field hospital, forcing it to close temporarily. When it was safe again, she and the others would return. Samuel would not be with them. He had a position at one of the hospitals in the capital city and had only been visiting the field hospital as part of a humanitarian volunteer corps. Doctors in the corps rotated in and out every two weeks. Zoe had met him at the field hospital the year before. After that they had exchanged sporadic letters. When she was sent to wait out the fighting, he had made the offer that she stay with him.

He was a gentle lover. The gentlest man she had ever known. She said it was because he was a surgeon, which made him laugh. "Surgeons aren't known for their tenderness." He said little about himself. She knew almost nothing about his family. He had a mother and a sister living somewhere in the city, but he had never introduced her to them. She knew he never would. They would not understand about her. When

63

Samuel married, Zoe knew, he would marry a woman he could take home, someone his mother and sister would approve. She knew that he would not marry for love. He did not look at marriage in the same way she did. He would marry as a duty, as a life ritual for having children; he would marry within the system in which he lived. This was how he defined personal satisfaction. She knew these things about him without being told.

Try as she might, though, she could not understand what had just happened in this kitchen with the boy in the band uniform. Nor could she quite understand the rage she suddenly felt. "I'm sick of this passive bullshit," she said. Her face flushed with anger. She wanted to keep going. "If you won't help that boy, I will." As she headed toward the door, prepared to leave in search of the boy, William and James abruptly stopped their clowning. They seemed frightened for her, though neither of them said anything. They looked to Samuel then. Samuel's expression was resigned. "Zoe. Have you heard nothing I've said? I can't let you go. The boy would associate you with my house, and I can't bring that trouble to my home."

"He didn't even see me," Zoe said.

"Of course he saw you. He saw everything. Nothing escaped his notice. He is a desperate boy. That uniform you so admire is the mark of just how desperate, how ruthless he is."

"I've never seen you be so unfair, Samuel," Zoe said and she started to cry. "That boy can't be more than twelve years old. How can you of all people believe a twelve-year-old boy capable of ruthlessness?"

Samuel raised his eyebrows, and she knew what the gesture meant. She had seen for herself just how cruel children could be. For the past two years she had witnessed their work. The fighting had been at the hands of children, boys younger than the one in the band uniform. She had seen atrocities that she would never forget. These images she kept tightly gathered in her subconscious, sealed away, and now that Samuel reminded her, she could not pretend she had not seen the work of thuggish boys: mutilations, torture, assassinations. Samuel didn't need to say it, but he said it anyway, "You think the fighting is just there with guns? You think it's all contained there? You know better than that, Zoe."

His saying it out loud was how she knew the depth of his disappointment in her. She could see it, too, in the way he turned his back to her and began to clean up. Samuel was not the sort of man to explain things. Zoe knew Samuel had especially resented having to say what he had in front of William and James. His shame was for her, not himself. William and James were still sober. The laughter had ceased. All of them, she sensed, were taking stock of something, weighing something—her risk to them.

She had been trained; it was there in all the training. Do not get involved too deeply with the local population. The risk had always been described in terms of her safety, but anyone would have known it was not just her safety in question. The trainers, whether they intended it or not, were protecting others as well, those who did not have powerful diplomats to intercede on their behalf; those who had no place to run if the fighting got too bad, who received no shipments of goods if they were cold or hungry; those who had no possibility of being airlifted out of the country if their lives were in danger.

She would eat this last meal with Samuel and his friends. They would eat together as the sun went down, dipping their bread into the savory stew one last time. They would laugh and joke together, and the boy in the band uniform would not be mentioned. And then she would go. She would not wait to be asked. Samuel knew this about her. At least she would not need to be asked to go.

She would make her way then, alone, through the quiet city streets carrying her bag. Samuel would not say goodbye. He would not offer to accompany her to the compound, temporary quarters, where she would sign in to stay until word came that it was safe to return to her work.

The Shouting Woman

Out the bay windows that night overlooking our back-yard, orange leaves from the maple trees fell slowly. My mother was telling a story as we sat at the dining room table.

"They're having a mouse problem. Both Mary Lou and Tom are afraid of mice," she explained, as though this somehow made them special comrades since they shared her fear of mice. Tom and Mary Lou McCoy were new teachers at the local high school and had recently moved into the large house across the alley from us. I was most interested in them because of their one-and-a-half-year-old son, Buster. "Even Tom is afraid," my mother went on. "He won't release the traps after they've been caught." Daddy shook his head as he bent to take a bite of sauerkraut and sausage. "Mary Lou says they can barely stand to sweep the traps into the dust pan, and they fight over who did it last, taking turns."

Daddy shook his head again. "I never." He liked Tom, but I could tell that my father, a working man, never really trusted a man who didn't work with his hands. In Tom's case, since he coached the local football and track teams in addition to teaching chemistry, Daddy seemed to have made an exception. My parents had sort of adopted Tom and Mary Lou, and already after living near us for less than four months it was common for one or the other of them to come to our house for advice, or to borrow a tool, or an appliance. In addition, Mom had started babysitting Buster while Mary Lou and Tom were teaching all day. I had been told that the following year I would be old enough to babysit. Only the Saturday before, Mary Lou had paid me to come watch Buster while she did some house cleaning. Often, during the hours between his parents' arrival home and the supper hour on those fall days, I played with Buster in our back yard where Mary Lou could watch from the kitchen window as she prepared their meal. She had told my mother that she didn't know how she'd managed without having me next door and that once I was twelve she'd hire me to babysit on weekend evenings.

"What they need is a good mouser," Daddy said that night, "like that big old tom we used to have." I had already finished my meal and wanted to leave the table. My younger brothers were wrestling with one another in their chairs. My mother had already scolded them a couple of times, when Daddy shouted, "Stop that goofing around! Get out of here! All of you!" He looked at me then, "It's okay if you stay, Jenny." I was often singled out in this way because I was the oldest child, and the only girl.

"That's okay," I said.

I pushed my chair away from the table, but before I left I heard Daddy say to Mom under his breath, "They might want to get thicker walls over there too."

"Shush now," Mom said. I didn't know what Daddy meant and didn't care. I was anxious to get to my bedroom and close the door. My room was large, with a dormer window facing south toward the alley that ran behind our house. I could see the top of the McCoy's roof above the trees. The walls of my room had been painted a pale pink that summer, and my mother had made a flouncy pink floral bedspread and matching curtains. I plunked down on the bed to read my newest Nancy Drew mystery, *Nancy Drew and the Hidden Staircase*. Each Saturday I walked downtown to the one-room library in our small town. I liked it best in winter with the tangy smell of propane heat and the dusty smell of old leather books. I had secretly begun to refer to myself as a sleuth, something Nancy was called. It was a word I admired but didn't really know how to pronounce, so I kept it to myself as I did all of my mystery solving aspirations.

As I tried to read that evening I kept hearing intermittent bumps of what I guessed were shoes or elbows coming from my brothers' bedroom. My brothers were on strict orders from both of my parents not to enter my room. Mom referred to the boys a herd of locust.

They were muscular and short, all three of them almost the same size. Daddy took out his clippers each week and buzzed their heads into crew cuts. They were all one year apart in age, though people often thought they were triplets, an illusion furthered by my mother's habit of dressing them all alike: Wrangler blue jeans and striped T-shirts. Their bedroom housed a set of bunk beds and a single bed between which they constantly rotated. My parents need not have bothered with the beds, though, for every morning, despite starting out in the bedroom, we found them asleep in various parts of the house: curled beneath the kitchen table, across the threshold to the bathroom, sprawled in the middle of the living room floor. They never remembered how they had gotten out of their beds in the night, but to a boy they were never there in the morning. The boys were like a separate species, a triple-headed hydra, inseparable and almost indistinguishable.

Little Buster loved the boys, and when they came home from school he struggled to keep up with them. "Wait, boys," he would say. "Come on, little fella," one of them invariably called over his shoulder. They didn't mean to leave him, but they had too much to do in their spare time after school. They had things to burn and things to tear down. All of this was small consolation to Buster, who was left with no one better to play with than me.

It was never long after we were home from school before his mother, always Mary Lou alone, came to pick him up. I thought Mary Lou was beautiful. As the weather got colder, she wore a leopard print car coat and a black beret. Her auburn hair curled about her face; her large brown eyes always smiled beneath her wispy bangs. When I wasn't reading that winter I began the habit of staring at myself in the mirror of my vanity dresser, willing myself to be as elegant as Mary Lou.

Without fail, when Mary Lou came in the door each day to pick him up, Buster pitched a fit, as though punishing her for having left him.

"Does he do this all day?" she asked my mother, every day embarrassed all over again by his bad behavior.

"Are you kidding?" Mom would say. "We wouldn't still be taking him if he did. No, he's awfully good. It's just that when you come home he doesn't know who's in charge anymore. Kids like to know there's an adult in charge. It makes them feel safe." She said almost the same thing every day, and Mary Lou, as though hearing it for the first time, was always reassured.

"Thank you, Carolyn," she said, and I could tell she meant it. "I don't know what I would have done if we hadn't met you when we moved here. I'd be going out of my mind right now."

Adults were strange to me in their need to repeat themselves. My parents talked about the same topics over and over, the weather, the local sports teams, the price of food and utilities. I was puzzled and bored by most of their talk, but now and then something changed in their tone. They lowered their voices slightly. It was clear at those times they didn't want my brothers or me to hear what it was they were discussing. Because of Nancy Drew, I knew it was important to pay attention, and I tried whenever possible to listen to those conversations. I had found that if I appeared to be engrossed in something else, my parents often talked in my presence. That was how I first knew there was some problem between Mary Lou and Tom. I couldn't understand what the problem was, but my parents seemed concerned.

Only one time that year did Mary Lou wonder if my mother was the best babysitter for Buster. It happened after school when my mother was trusting my brothers and me to be watching out for him. My brothers had been quiet for a long time that mild day in early winter, never a good sign, and my mother had sent Buster and me out to look for them. We found them not far away on a small mound in a field around the corner from our house. They were throwing something from off the top of the mound. Each time they threw, they ducked, and there followed a small explosion. Not until Buster and I got closer did I realize they were throwing little bombs they had made out of dried gourds from the garden. They later called them Molotov cocktails. While I was busy scolding the boys, Buster lifted to his mouth a box of gunpowder the boys had brought with them. Kevin, the oldest of my brothers, shouted at him, "Buster, put that down!" It was so rare for one of the boys to directly address Buster and especially in such a forthright, deliberate way, that Buster immediately pulled the box away from his mouth. I rushed to him.

"Did you eat some?" He shook his head but the strong black powder was all over his face and down his shirt, and there was no way to be sure. "Now, see what you've done," I said to the boys. "If you wouldn't pull these stunts . . ."

None of them said anything in response to me, but they silently followed me home. I had seen the crisis as an excuse to carry Buster and he was unusually compliant as I lugged him awkwardly, stopping frequently to shift his weight from one hip to the other. His submission to this uncomfortable trip was a testament to my anger. All of them were a bit in awe of me that day, and it was the first glimpse I had of the power of my will.

My mother met us in the yard and took Buster from me. She checked him hurriedly, assuming he had been injured. "He ate gunpowder," I said.

"How'd he get hold of it?" My mother interrogated the boys even as she moved into the house to call the doctor. Later, when the story was retold to Mary Lou, my mother kept some of the details from her. We were fortunate that Buster had not eaten any of the gunpowder, but still I saw a trace of doubt in Mary Lou's eyes as Mother told her the story. It was a long time before I was asked again to come over and watch him as I had in the weeks previous.

Later that winter I began to wake up in the night. I didn't know what was waking me at first and easily fell back to sleep, but as the pattern persisted, it became difficult for me to sleep once I'd been awakened. Just after Christmas, I got up one night and in the dark crept downstairs to the bathroom. I tripped over my brother Mark, who was asleep in the hall. "Go back to bed," I said and nudged him awake with my foot. "Go on back to bed." He stood up groggily and half asleep went back to his bedroom. While I was in the bathroom, I heard a strange noise. Eventually I realized it was the sound of muffled shouting. I couldn't make out if it was a man or a woman, and when I looked out the bathroom window I saw nothing. It wasn't until I was in the kitchen that I noticed the light in the McCoy's house. Before I went back to bed, my mother came into the kitchen.

"What are you doing up?" she said, not in the least startled to see me standing there by the sink.

"Something woke me."

"Yes, I imagine," she said. "Try to go back to sleep now."

In the months to come I was awakened perhaps once a week and each time it was the same, someone shouting, and the light there in the McCoy's house. I was inspired to go out to investigate finally one night in February. I remember thinking to myself, "What would Nancy do?" as I put on my clothes over my flannel night gown and left the house to get closer to the shouting. The shades were all drawn in the upstairs rooms of the McCoy house where the light was. The nearer I got to the house the more distinct the shouting. Even though I could hear her words, I couldn't understand what Mary Lou was shouting. Mainly, she was laughing, a sort of crying laugh, and her voice sounded raggedy and hoarse. "You. You," she said over and over. I never heard anything from Tom and wondered if maybe she was talking to herself. I stepped farther back in the yard so I could see more of the windows, hoping I might see a shadow behind the shades, but I saw nothing. The thought occurred to me as I began to feel miserable with cold and exhaustion that Nancy Drew would find some way to get inside the house to investigate further. When it came right down to it, I realized I didn't have the nerve to do it myself.

Through the long summer when everyone's windows were open, I expected to hear the shouting again and had plans in the warmer weather to be a real sleuth. I called it the Case of the Shouting Woman and narrated possible scenarios to myself. Strangely, though, through that entire summer I was never once awakened by the shouting in the night. We saw Buster now and then but not every day as we did while his parents were working during the school year. Mary Lou often waved from the alley or came over to borrow something, but we saw little of them otherwise. I was glad when school started again and Buster was at our house each day. I had turned twelve. Mary Lou did not forget her promise and told me she was as pleased as I was now that I could babysit. "Tom and I are looking forward to going on dates again," she told me.

I wasn't really babysitting that day. It was early November, chilly but sunny. I had been outside raking leaves and Mary Lou asked if Buster could come over for awhile, just so she could run to the store. "Mousetraps." She laughed and waved a ten-dollar bill she took from her jeans' pocket. "Lots of them," she said. Buster fell into the leaves I had piled and began to fling handfuls into the air. "Yippee, yippee," he said.

I watched Mary Lou walk away down the rutted alley toward the highway a few blocks away where she would have to cross to get to the stores downtown. She wore a lightweight navy blue jacket and swung her arms freely. I admired how pretty she was, dreaming of my own future when I too would be a teacher, married to a handsome man, the mother of a little boy of my own.

Buster had started to complain about the cold when my mother called about an hour later. The sun was setting and a harvest moon bobbed on the eastern horizon. "See the big moon," I said and pointed for Buster.

"Balloon," he said, his eyes wide.

"No, the moon." Buster frowned as I said this.

"Jenny," my mother called again. She stretched my name out "Jeeeeeeneeeee" and it floated across the clear thin air of the evening. I felt it traveling across the roofs of the houses out of the neighborhood, all the way to the store where Mary Lou must have met someone and had a long conversation.

"Mary Lou asked me to watch Buster while she went to buy mousetraps," I explained to my mother. Mother looked down the same rutted alley where Mary Lou had gone. She frowned. "How long ago?"

"Maybe an hour?"

"Dinner's almost ready. Buster will just have to eat with us." Hearing his name Buster began to throw handfuls of leaves again. My mother chased him playfully and tickled him. He spun in the orange leaves, his giggles making my mother laugh. She pulled him to his feet and hugged him. "You're going to come eat with us, Munchkin."

"I not a Munchkin."

"You're not? What are you?"

"I a boy."

"Oh," my mother said. "We like to eat little boys at our house." And she chased him to the house, Buster shrieking in delight if she got too close. Before they made it into the backdoor though, Tom honked and waved as he pulled into their drive.

"You go on in and get the table set." My mother gestured to me as she turned to walk Buster to his house. When he saw Tom, Buster took off across the yard. "Daddy, Daddy."

"Hey, big guy," Tom said and lifted him up. I could smell my mother's famous ham and sweet potato casserole as I went in the back door.

Shortly after supper that night the phone rang. It was Tom. My mother covered the mouthpiece. "What time did Mary Lou leave this afternoon?" she asked me.

"About 4:30," I said, and for some reason I didn't understand, I felt my heart plummet.

"I can't think what might have happened," my mother was saying, and then, "No, you're right. It's not at all like her." By now Daddy had gone to stand beside Mom. Even the boys, who had been building a complicated fort under the dining room table, stopped their chatter and listened. It felt in that moment as though the whole family had stopped breathing, joined together by a tension we couldn't describe, a string suddenly pulled tight. The clock on the mantle in the living room ticked.

"Let me talk to him." Daddy nudged my mother. And then we could all breathe again.

"She's not back?" I said once my mother was off the phone.

"No." She didn't look at me, seemed distracted and impatient. "She never went to the store."

"Never went . . .? But I watched her . . . she had $10.00 . . . She said mousetraps."

Mom put the tablecloth back on the dining room table. I helped her smooth it, all the while repeating silently to myself "mousetraps, mousetraps, mousetraps, mousetraps."

Daddy's low rumble was unintelligible, so we didn't learn anything from what he said until he was off the phone. "No one saw her downtown," he said. "Tom's called the area hospitals, the police. Nothing." Daddy looked away for awhile. "You don't suppose . . . ?" he started.

"No," my mother said.

Then both of my parents turned their attention to me, a very keen, adult attention that frightened me.

"Was she carrying anything?"

"What exactly was she wearing?"

"Did she seem strange?"

"You're sure she didn't have a purse?"

"Was there a possibility she had a bag that she picked up later?"

"How did she seem?"

"Say once again exactly what she said."

When later the local sheriff came by he asked me those same questions, and then Tom after him. There was no longer any pretense I was a child. I was the only witness, the last person to have seen Mary Lou before she what? Disappeared? Ran away? Left? Was kidnapped? The possibilities seemed endless suddenly, each one more awful than the next. What unspeakable crime may have been committed? Now that there was a real mystery to solve I was disappointed by how horrible it felt, how much I didn't want to be a part of it in any way, how much my mind refused to speculate and analyze the way Nancy Drew's did.

In the days to come men from neighboring counties came to search the surrounding area. The ditches for miles along the highway were gone over inch by inch. Maybe she'd been hit. They were looking for her clothing, too, in case of what they called foul play. Nothing. Bloodhounds and more search parties. For the next several weeks, very little was talked about except what might have happened to Mary Lou. Sometime in the middle of the search Daddy, along with almost everyone else in town, resigned himself to the fact that Mary Lou had left on her own volition, while my mother insisted that she wouldn't do that. "She couldn't have gone off and left that child. No matter what else she might have been thinking, she could not have left that child. I would have known if she was planning something like that." I believed my mother's confident assurances, for I too couldn't imagine how Mary Lou could have left Buster. To myself sometimes I called Mary Lou's disappearance the Case of the Missing Woman, but as the weeks went on I surprised myself with my lack of desire to try to solve the mystery. I had no sense of where to begin, what questions to ask.

Mary Lou was the subject of every conversation, all anyone could talk about. The rumors were often vicious, and I heard it all, every shocking adult speculation, so strangely cruel and childish. I was surprised and disappointed by their pettiness. Adults didn't know more or better than children. I understood that then. And I understood other things as well: Tom was a drinker. Mary Lou was subject to fits of rage, some said on the verge of a breakdown. Tom was a "stick in the mud," Mary Lou was a "firecracker." Their marriage was in deep trouble. There were other women and other men.

Buster stayed at our house more than usual, but the boys, now sensing the gravity of the situation, had taken him into their boys' world, and I lost Buster at that time as much as I lost Mary Lou. I felt strangely alone in the family—my parents had each other, and the boys and Buster were a world unto themselves. I felt unmoored, and in the context of that emotion I thought about the possibilities of walking out of one life and into another, leaving one identity and simply picking up a new one. I couldn't even read my Nancy Drew mysteries. The frightening situations were more than I could bear when I suddenly had, as I had once so dearly wished, a real mystery of my own to solve. Had Mary Lou just left? I had no sense as I played back to myself again and again my last conversation with her that she was not planning to come back. I went over and over again in my mind the details of that last conversation, wondering if I was in some way not remembering clearly, and I always came back to the same thing: she hadn't looked like someone saying goodbye.

It was my conviction about the sincerity of Mary Lou's last words that kept Tom searching. He seemed to need to talk to me periodically, to hear me repeat that, no, I didn't think she had intended to leave, nor did I think her reference to mousetraps was intended as a coded message the way some people in town apparently did. I listened to the ways my words, Mary Lou's words, were taken up and perverted by rumor and nuance. I heard the words after they'd made the transit, heavy now with innuendo and inflection, like a barnacle encrusted rock, much of the meaning of which escaped me at the time.

Once the official search was called off that winter everyone, except Tom and me, seemed to lose energy for the question of Mary Lou. Everyone seemed relieved to go back to their normal lives. I had started to babysit more for Tom, especially on weekends when he had ball games to coach and we talked about little else. When he came home late after those ball games, Tom offered me a soft drink and poured himself a large glass of whiskey. He sat on the couch across from the chair where I always sat and watched TV after Buster had gone to bed. He wanted to talk. It was always the same.

"How'd the team do?" I'd say.

"They played their damnedest," he'd answer, and I never knew if that was a good or a bad thing until he recapped the game. I never interrupted. He talked, and I listened.

Then he would grow quiet and sink deeper into the couch, holding the glass between his knees so that his shoulders seemed to curl inward. He looked tired and old; his eyes changed and I barely recognized him. Then he talked again. I knew enough after awhile to wait, not to get in a hurry to leave during this time, because he wanted me to stay, not to say anything, just to listen. My conversations with Tom reminded me of those between my parents. Over and over again, the same themes, the same questions and reassurances. How many times did I say, "they'll find her for sure"?

I knew my parents didn't approve of Tom keeping me out so late on those weekend nights, and when Mom threatened to talk to him about it I felt slightly frantic and begged her to drop it. I needed those conversations as much as Tom did. The way Tom and I saw it, either Mary Lou was alive or she was dead. Either she didn't want to be with her family or she was desperate to get back, needing help of some kind. Neither possibility was a happy prospect, and I could see why those questions might drive someone round the bend. I could see why Tom might start neglecting Buster as he did. I could understand why there were complaints from parents at school about his drinking, but I never could understand why Tom sold the house and moved away with Buster as soon as school was out that spring.

That summer their house sat empty, I began to wake in the night again. I sat in our dark dining room and watched the McCoy house through the trees, never feeling alone, for though they were sleepwalkers, my brothers were always asleep somewhere nearby, their bodies shining and still in the rays of silver moonlight coming through the windows, like old statues, like pictures I had seen of the residents of an ancient city surprised and stopped by a volcanic eruption.

I watched through the dark, my eyes aching, willing Mary Lou back, and after weeks of watching, one night in August my vigil was rewarded when I saw someone standing in the McCoy's back yard. Without a doubt I knew it was Mary Lou. I ran outside in my pajamas, my bare feet scraping against the gravel and dirt clods in the alley. The summer night was humid and misty, the grass of the McCoy's lawn damp with dew. I was not prepared when I reached their yard to find no one was there. The moon was bright and I could see clearly the empty house and the silent yard. I wondered why Mary Lou would run away from me. After I had circled the house several times, maybe I even called her name, I told myself that maybe Mary Lou was hiding for a reason, and I gave up and went back home. Daddy was standing at the backdoor in his boxer shorts, his bare feet very white in the moonlight.

"What are you thinking, running around the neighborhood this time of the night?" He frowned as he opened the screen door for me.

"I saw Mary Lou." I turned to point over my shoulder toward the McCoy's. "She was standing in their backyard." My father shook his head and frowned. I knew he didn't believe me, but I noticed in spite of that he craned his neck a little to look toward the McCoy's as he stepped back to let me in.

"Have you been doing this a lot?" he asked.

"Tonight's the first time I saw anything."

"So you have been watching?"

I nodded.

"You know Mary Lou's not coming back, don't you?"

I shook my head. "She will. That was her just now. She's afraid, not knowing where Tom and Buster are, but she'll come back."

"Oh, darlin'." Daddy gathered me into his arms. His bristly chest hair tickled my cheek. "This is a nasty old business. A kid shouldn't have to be caught up in something like this. You know if Mary Lou wants to find Tom and Buster, she will. She'll know how. You don't have to watch out for her. She's a grown woman."

What I could never tell Daddy that night, what I had told no one, was how I thought had made Mary Lou disappear. I hadn't wished her dead, hadn't wished her *really* gone, hadn't wished her ill at all, for I loved Mary Lou, but I had wished her away and wished myself into her place. It had only been a fleeting thought. Such a little thing. How could such a little thought be so powerful? But hadn't it happened just as I'd wished? Hadn't I taken care of Buster, and hadn't Tom sought me out, preferred me to others? Hadn't Mary Lou disappeared?

No, my father couldn't have begun to understand my fears on that night. I envied my mother her fear of mice. What I feared was myself and my own capricious desires. Through that long summer what I had done each night as I watched in the darkness was the equivalent of prayer—urging my mind to a solitary thought, undoing a terrible wrong, a mistake I had made. I concentrated all of my will toward bringing Mary Lou back from wherever I thought I had inadvertently sent her.

I never saw Mary Lou again, though I continued to watch most nights until school started again that fall. A funny thing happened in that last week before school started again. My brothers stopped sleepwalking. The first night it happened, I walked through the house looking for them, convinced they must have gotten past me somehow. But there they were, all of them still snug in their beds. It happened the next night, and the next. No one could account for why they had stopped, just as no one could account for why they had sleepwalked in the first place.

When the orange maple leaves fell thick between our yards, and I turned thirteen, the Murphys with their two dogs, three cats, numerous birds, and seven kids, moved into the McCoy house. The neighborhood was filled with the happy uproar of that big family, and I was seduced by the distraction. I happily let the Murphys with their mad, lively, chaos, and their son Jeremy, sweep away my vigil and my memory of Mary Lou.

Miss Kielbasa

When my mother called to ask if I'd come home to help my brother, Doug, prepare for his first year competing in the annual queen contest, a part of my hometown's summer festival, I told her I didn't want to do it. Each year my dad goes all out for the contest. He won it once, the year after Doug was born, and he wants to be the first man in the contest's recorded history to win twice. My mother, who always has her hands full helping Dad, said to me, "Diane, I can't help both of them. It's a conflict of interest." Like it wasn't a conflict of interest for me to help out? I wasn't interested. That was the main conflict. But, it's traditional for eighteen-year-olds to compete in their first year of eligibility— not just a tradition, downright traitorous if they don't— and there's an unspoken rule in town that a man who won't take part in the queen contest is a man you can't trust.

Plus, I knew my brother, Doug, and I figured he'd have plans for the $2,000 cash prize for winning.

Thanks to Eman Grant, who left $30,000 when he died in 1982 to "ensure that the contest would survive into the next century."

So, I took time off from my job in Lincoln as an administrative assistant at the Arbor Day Foundation and came home a week ago to help Doug get ready, only my mother didn't entirely trust that I could do it. Two days after I arrived she asked, "Does he have a good razor?" She made a point of not looking at my own unshaven legs and underarms.

"I brought one with me," I said.

She seemed surprised but not overly impressed. "He has all the proper underthings: slip? Bra? Nylons?" An inventory I've been known to neglect in my own apparel. I'm a disappointment to my mother: overweight, hair any color but my own. She thinks I'm craving attention.

I reassured her, "We found everything in Kearney at the second-hand stores." I leaned closer then, as though to confide. "We even found a pair of high heels to fit." My mother beamed and I nodded again. "He's learning to walk in them."

"That's wonderful," she said, obviously relieved.

I had asked Donnell not to contact me while I was at home, but he called the first night anyway. "I thought I told you not to call me," I said.

"Yeah, and I think I won't be offended by that," he answered. He doesn't understand anything. He doesn't understand, for instance, that if my parents found out he was black . . . well, I don't know what would happen. I don't want to know.

He used to get angry when I said things like that but now he laughs. "It's illegal to lynch a black man these days," he says. I don't know how he can be so flippant. Then he goes on, "My family wasn't too keen on your white hide either, but I figured that was their problem, and now they accept you just fine."

I insist that it's different with my family, as though white people can hold grudges longer, or that prejudice going that direction is worse. Donnell says I'm full of shit when I say things like that. He thinks the sooner my family starts adjusting to the idea of us being together the better. We're getting married next year, and I'm still trying to decide whether I'll tell the folks or let them find out the hard way on the day of the wedding. It won't be a traditional wedding anyway. "Not an option," Donnell tells me.

Donnell thinks this whole queen contest is hilarious. He's completely jazzed about the idea of all these small town guys—farmers, mechanics, teachers, the principal of the high school, the Lutheran minister, the banker, the mortician—all in drag. He wanted to come with me this year to see the competition, but I told him no. "No way."

My brother Doug is very handsome. He got Mom's good looks. Tall, high cheekbones, good body. I took after my father, squatty and big featured. Maybe that's why I don't bother with all those feminine pretensions. Donnell protests about my self image, says I have it all wrong, that I'm pretty in a natural way. "Sure, you're not the poster girl for white bread America, but that's good. Right?" He's nice for saying it.

I expected Doug would be beautiful in drag, but was I ever wrong. He is one ugly woman. We laughed ourselves silly after we finally got him all decked out: an auburn wig cut in layers to his shoulders, a royal blue satin dress with a sweetheart neckline, black heels, white rhinestone necklace and earrings. Makeup. The whole deal. And then, walking in high heels. The first time he tried he wobbled, bent double, and threw his arms out for balance. The bottom of the tight dress kept yanking short his stride. He got so frustrated at one point he tore off the wig and the earrings. "I'm not doing this," he said. "I'm not entering this bullshit contest."

I let him fume for awhile and then I handed him back his wig. "If you ever want to show your face in this town again you will." And that's the truth of it. Doug knew it too. He sighed and put the wig back on. There's the big way that Doug and I are different. Doug loves this place. It would kill him if the people here disapproved of him. He's got a job at the grain elevator and he wants to stay there.

Yesterday morning I got up early for some reason, probably all the birds in our backyard. Little bastards. I decided to join Doug and Dad for coffee and cinnamon rolls at Leona's cafe downtown. Most of the men of the town gather there before work on week days. The only other women were Leona and the two waitresses: Kit and Julie. I felt a little funny as I walked in, like maybe I was breaking a rule or something.

"Hey, stranger," several of the men said to me. I sat with Doug and Dad on one of the red vinyl stools at the counter, and I couldn't help remembering how as a little kid walking to school I would look through the windows of the cafe every morning and see all the men of my town sitting there together. From where I sat at the counter, I could see through the smudged windows the tall white bins of the elevator. They seemed to tilt slightly in the blue sky, wisps of clouds like haloes. I contemplated for a moment what a nice photograph that might be.

Doug was looking at me. "What are you staring at?"

"The site of your brilliant career in grain," I said.

He smiled. He thinks that makes perfect sense.

Some of the older men started teasing Doug then about it being his first year out. "Here he is, Miss Crazy Days," one of them sang. Doug hopped down off his stool when he heard that and sashayed around the diner with one hand on his hip, the other raised in 'the wave.' He'd told me that for the last few weeks all the guys around town had been greeting each other in their cars and trucks with "the wave" rather than their usual one or two finger off the steering wheel greeting.

Ben Jurgens walked into the cafe just as Doug had

started his little performance. He waited for a while before saying, "that your idea of 'the walk'? Ben is a big man with a huge belly that he rubs affectionately as though it isn't a part of himself but rather a pet or a child. "Now this is 'the walk,'" he said. He pulled his hips forward, and with surprising grace pranced about the diner.

"Why don't you sit down, Jurgens," Leona said in her whiskey voice from behind the counter. "Before you make everybody sick first thing this morning."

"Oooh," several guys said anticipating Ben's response to Leona's challenge.

"Not before everyone sees what I'm doing for my talent tomorrow night." With that, he lifted his shirt to expose his hairy belly. He rocked his hips and his belly began to undulate. We were all a little mesmerized by the sight of that belly. Finally everyone groaned, and Ben, satisfied with the response, went to sit down.

"How you doin', Diane?" Leona said as she set a cup of coffee on the counter.

"I'm okay."

"You don't look too happy to be back."

I shrugged. "I'm okay."

Leona nodded toward Doug. "You making that brother of yours beautiful?"

"I'm doing the best I can with what I have."

"Isn't that the truth," Leona said. "Isn't that what we're all doing."

My father, his mouth slightly full of cinnamon roll,

said, "Some of us have better luck in that department than others."

I couldn't believe it when I got back home later that morning and my mother said, "A friend of yours called while you were gone. A fellow named Donnell."

"Oh," I said, hoping I sounded nonchalant even though I felt like wringing his neck. I knew he was doing it deliberately, putting me in a bad situation.

"I miss you, sweetie," he said when I called him back later. "Really." But he was laughing. He's been trying anything he can to out our relationship to my parents. "Two years is a long time," he said to me. He thinks it's so simple. Now, he's finally decided that I need help, that I'll never do it on my own. I insist he needs to give me more time, let me do it my way. "What way is that, Diane?" he said. "It doesn't look like any way I've ever seen."

"How's Doug doing?" he asked me.

"Fine."

He pressed me for details, and I could hear him dying laughing on the other end of the line. I played it up a bit, described what had happened earlier that morning with Ben in the diner. He loved it. "I want to enter this contest," he said. "After we get married can I qualify as a contestant?"

I didn't want to say anything, but suddenly I was picturing it—Donnell in a dress and everyone staring, silent, their mouths open, not because they've never seen a man in a dress, but because they've never seen a black man close up before. I didn't tell him any of that, and maybe he wouldn't believe me anyway, but he ought to. It's the truth.

My mother had the stereo playing in the background. She loves Kenny G., Yanni, John Tesh. All day long she plays their CDs over and over. Donnell overheard John Tesh singing "God Bless America," and started singing along. That's when I told him I had to go. I felt caught in the middle when he started to make fun. It's all the more reason Donnell can't meet my family for a while longer. I have to protect them from him, too.

When I got off the phone, Mom was in the kitchen kneading bread. Her women's group from the Catholic church, the Miriam Circle, always has a fundraiser booth at the festival where they sell food. I sat down at the table and played with the pink Melmac salt and pepper shakers while Mom formed the dough into little rolls

"So, is Donnell a good friend?" my mother said. Her voice had that lilt to it, the edge of teasing. They're always after me about having a boyfriend, afraid perhaps that I'll never have one, or, horrors, that I don't like men at all.

I shrugged.

"I take that to mean he's more than a friend."

"Back off, Mom."

She lifted her dough-covered hands in surrender

and then washed off at the sink. "I want to show you what I did this morning while you were gone." She's good like that, changing the subject without getting too ruffled. She disappeared down the hall, and when she came back she was carrying one of the little teddy bears she collects. It was dressed like a queen, but she had added a tiny beard and mustache so there would be no question what kind of queen it was.

"Mother," I said when I saw the bear.

"Isn't it darling?"

"It's nuts."

Mom looked at the little bear with a smile. "I know," she said, still smiling as she turned the bear toward her. "But the ladies from Circle will love it."

And they did. Later, when all of them arrived they squealed and exclaimed over the teddy bear. "It's darling, Linda. It's just darling." My mother basked in the glow of their approval. Oh, don't get me wrong. She's adorable, my mother. I had to shake my head as I watched her there among her friends. They were meeting to discuss the booth—who'd do what, when—but most of them had also brought along last minute sewing projects, costumes for their sons and husbands for the following night.

Jean Warren was attaching a ruffle to the bottom of a large white bathing suit to which she had already added ample insets. "I'm really down to the wire getting this done," she said. She held it up, and we could all picture her husband James, the bank president, a rather pudgy balding man ordinarily seen only in suits and ties, wearing the white swimsuit.

That night after Doug got home from work we went through his talent act one more time, an old aerobics routine I'd learned in a class I'd taken at the YWCA the year before. He hammed it up, even pulling my old sombrero from where it had been hanging for years on the mirror of my dresser, and putting it on. We decided it would be a good addition for the next night. "You're going to do fine," I said, and I actually envied him a little his confidence.

I wasn't happy to wake at 6:30 this morning to Mom pounding around in the kitchen and Dad mowing the lawn. I sat at the kitchen table, and listened to Mom talk about how there had been so many people at the festival the night before they'd run out of food at their booth and the entire Circle would have to cook all morning to have enough for that night.

She was reaching for another cup of flour when she noticed Doug standing in the doorway, hair on end, wearing only his boxers.

"You look terrible," she said.

"I feel like the entire Mongolian army marched across my tongue in their muddy boots."

"Oh, the Mongols. I guess I don't have to ask what the two of you did last night?"

"We just hung out," I said.

"Did you hang out in the bottom of a beer barrel?"

"It's just a phase we're going through." Doug poured himself a bowl of Cheerios and sat down beside me. I can't imagine how anyone can eat so early in the morning.

Donnell is a morning person. He's always wanting to take me out for breakfast, likes to find some out-of-the-way diner and get there early. I make him furious if I dawdle around. "What's the point of eating breakfast at 10:00?" he wonders. He wonders that because he can't imagine eating lunch at 3:00 and dinner at 9:00. He can't imagine eating when you feel hungry. He's strict about things like that, schedules and all, but he has to be. He's the second string violin for the Lincoln Symphony Orchestra, and he wants to be first violin within the next five years. He practices at least four hours every day. My parents have seen Donnell and don't know it was significant. I took them to one of his concerts a year ago. They both commented, like I knew they would, that it was unusual to see a black man playing a violin. They completely embarrassed me that night clapping like morons, the only people in the whole silent auditorium to clap during the intervals of a three movement piece.

Later, I teased Donnell. "You'll know my family anywhere. They're the ones acting socially inappropriate." Donnell said I shouldn't be so hard on them, that it happens all the time. He has a big thing about hating art snobs, and he said their faux pas endeared them to him. So, now I console myself. At least my folks aren't art snobs.

My mother was telling Doug this morning about an Internet site she had found the night before after she got home. "It has nothing but patterns for commemorative bears."

"What was the best one?" Doug asked, having to tip his head back to talk because his mouth was full of Cheerios.

"There were too many to choose from, but now this morning when I tried to find the site again, I couldn't."

Doug stood up to rinse his bowl in the sink. He leaned close to Mom's ear and whispered. "That's the trouble with you insane people. Things that seem real in the night aren't there the next morning." Mom pushed him away, and he smiled. "I'll help you find it later," he said.

She smiled back at him, then her smile slipped. "I hope you aren't so worn out from last night that you won't do well in the pageant tonight."

"I've got everything under control," Doug said. Then he tripped dramatically in the threshold of the door. "Nothing to worry about."

My brother takes nothing seriously, and yet everything always works out for him. He wants nothing and gets everything. He'll be a slacker gone successful despite his best efforts. And I know in advance, as though I've read the last page of a book, that he'll win the contest tonight. Presto, changeo, he'll be up $2,000 bucks,

and everybody in town will love him all over again—
like they do anyone who wins the contest—like they've
loved Doug for being the quarterback on the football
team, the center on the basketball team, and the
pitcher on the baseball team. He's the homegrown,
small town ideal.

I half expected to hear from Donnell this afternoon
and stuck around the house because of it. I didn't want
Mom intercepting another call from him. I was a little
bit disappointed when he didn't call, but it didn't last
long because by 3:00 I was helping Doug get ready to
go to the pageant.

When we arrived at the Legion Club Hall at 5:30
there were already people gathering. From past con-
tests, I knew that the hall would be full to capacity as
early as 6:30, the big double doors in the back open so
latecomers could gather and watch from the street. A
three-foot high wooden stage had been erected at the
west end of the hall, the bottom draped in a heavy blue
velvet skirt made from the old high school stage curtains, and festooned with white satin rosettes. A lectern
for the announcer stood to the right on the stage, and a
ten-foot runway extended into the hall.

Chairs ringed the front and sides of the stage. The
judges' tables were situated at the front on either side
of the runway. Their chairs had been decorated with
smaller white rosettes, and name tags marked their
places. Women from the community are chosen each

year to judge the event, with the stipulation that they have no relative competing in the pageant.

Floyd Klein, who has been announcing the program for as long as anyone remembers, checked the sound system as The Little Polka Band tuned and warmed up their instruments. I noticed Carol Mashek was playing with them tonight. She sat in her wheelchair now and rippled through the notes on her accordion. They would play at intermission and for the dance afterward. Meanwhile, the contestants gathered in the kitchen of the hall. It was crowded back there. Most of the guys were cheerful, though it was obvious they were already sweating and miserable.

I helped Doug stuff his bra with pillow batting once he'd gotten dressed. He pulled his dress away where it clung to his sweaty skin. A heat rash covered his chest where he had shaved. "This sucks," he said.

I told Doug to take a couple of deep breaths. He did as I said, and I realized this was one of the things I loved most about my brother, his gentle compliance about life. I quickly checked his outfit. "Everything looks great. You'll do well tonight. You have a good shot at winning this thing. Okay?" Doug nodded.

He seemed vague then as he looked at the other men in the room with us. There were the men of our town decked out in wigs and earrings, dresses and heels. Some of them wore hats and others carried purses. He shook his head. "All these years I've been watching this contest and now here I am."

"I almost forgot," I said then, and pulled from the bag I had brought a satin ribbon for Doug to wear. "Miss Kielbasa," it read.

"Hey, thanks," he said as he draped it across his chest. He looked down at it. "How's it look?"

"Great."

When later Dad walked onto the stage in the pink chiffon dress that successfully hid the small ring of fat around his middle, I was amazed. He walked effortlessly on his high heels. I suppose Dad had been doing it all the years I had been watching the competition, but I hadn't appreciated what it meant until now. He executed sharp yet graceful turns, smiled at the judges, completely transformed by more than just makeup and accessories, and watching this I understood the secret was that right then my father really believed he was a woman.

Then it was Doug's turn. As he started up the steps to the stage, he had one brief wobble in his heels. My heart skipped a beat as I watched that wobbly beginning, but he soon put my mind at ease. Doug was enjoying himself, I could see. His talent act went well, and he made a successful change into the swimsuit.

Before the five finalists were announced there was an intermission during which the band played "The Beer Barrel Polka" and a few other favorite old tunes. The room was too crowded during intermission for anyone to dance, but many of the older women in the audience stood up and clapped and swayed along to the music, sometimes grabbing a grandchild with whom to dance in place. I was sitting with Mom, who kept waving across the room to people she knew.

Once the band had finished playing, Floyd took his place again behind the microphone and quieted the crowd. "Everyone, take your seats now. It's time to announce our four finalists and our winner."

Immediately, a hush fell over the restless crowd. "Could I have a drum roll, there, Bill?" Floyd said. Bill nodded toward the band's drummer, who played a tight roll on the snare drum.

"The judges tell me the decision tonight was very difficult. They wish to thank all of the contestants for their cooperation." A burst of applause from the audience interrupted Floyd momentarily. He didn't let it stop him for long. "Our fourth runner up tonight is Milo Vaschik." At the announcement, the drummer threw in a cymbal crash and then quieted as the crowd applauded. Once the applause had subsided, he began to build another drum roll.

"Our third runner up, folks, is . . ." the drum roll crescendoed as Floyd drew out the announcement. "Ben Jurgens."

The crowd burst into applause and laughter. Ben, wearing a red, two-piece, floor-length ensemble, came down the runway. He stopped, turned his back to the audience and coyly looked over his shoulder. Then he turned to face the audience again, lifted the top portion of his outfit, and once more regaled us with his belly dance. Everyone went wild, and the drummer did a number of cymbal crashes in quick succession.

"Now for the second runner up, everyone. Everyone," Floyd said and lifted his hands to quiet the audience. "Our second runner-up tonight, is . . . Larry Martin." Larry Martin is one of those men who is transformed every year into a beautiful woman during the pageant. Larry tends to place among the finalists in every competition, but somehow can never quite win the title. I saw now that it was because he didn't bother with certain feminine mannerisms, so that he seemed beautiful and at the same time rough and abrupt. He accepted the flowers Floyd handed him and nodded toward the audience.

"The contest got very close here, folks," Floyd said as he glanced to the remaining contestants. A few of them had to take one last chance to ham. Donald Meyers waved a white handkerchief toward Floyd. Elmer Yoder blew a kiss, while Jacob Zulko and Alan Slobavech hugged and mimicked high anxiety.

"Should anything happen to disqualify this year's reigning Crazy Day's Queen, our first runner up will step into the role." Floyd looked toward the band's drummer. "Could I have another drum roll there, Erwin?"

Erwin, slightly startled, began another drum roll. "Our first runner up tonight is . . . Bob Lewandowski." My father. Once again the crowd went wild. Dad is popular, a volunteer fireman, one of the guys everyone in town feels they can come to for help of any sort. At the announcement, Mom and I clasped hands.

"And now for the moment we've been waiting for." Floyd once again looked behind him toward the row of remaining contestants. "This is a bit unusual, folks, that someone has won the contest in their first year out, and I'm proud to announce that this year's queen is Doug Lewandowski." The audience leapt up, clapping and stomping as Doug went forward to accept the crown and the roses. He took his runway walk without a wobble anywhere and waved his perfect white-gloved hand, "the wave." To accompany him on his walk the band struck up their polkaized version of "Here She Comes, Miss America." Flashbulbs popped, and the crowd continued to clap and shout. Through it all Doug never lost his composure. I hugged Mom who wiped away tears. "Your father will be so proud."

I looked back to the stage, surprised to see Dad beaming toward Doug, obviously thrilled. "Isn't he disappointed? He always wants to win again."

Mom shook her head. Above the din of the crowd she said, "He wanted Doug to win. Couldn't you see that?"

"I give you once more," Floyd was saying across the PA system. "This year's reigning queen—Miss Kielbasa—Doug Lewandowski." Another roar from the crowd as this time people surged toward the front of the auditorium, Mom among them. I watched as people gathered around Doug. His wig was askew from the hugging, and his lipstick smeared as every woman in town kissed him. Eventually, when Doug stood up, I could see he was back to himself, just Doug, a slightly awkward teenage boy in a dress. He made eye contact with me and gave me the thumbs up sign. The band played, and while chairs were put away, dancers took up the space. Doug came down the stairs of the stage toward me. "My feet are killing me," he said as he kicked off his high heels.

I hugged him. "I'm so proud of you."

"Good coaching always shows." Doug held open his arms. "Watch that you don't step on my feet," he said as he whirled me in an energetic polka. Many of the other contestants, still in costume, also danced with wives and girlfriends.

"Hey, congratulations," they shouted above the music as Doug and I jostled through the crowd.

"So when do you get the check?" I asked.

"I've got it already." Doug indicated he had stuck it into his bra. He shrugged then. "I forgot to bring a purse." He paused. "Next year."

"Next year," I echoed.

As Doug led me in the polka he swung me near the double doors at the back of the hall, and that's when I saw Donnell standing in the open doorway. He smiled and waved at me. I froze.

"What's up?" Doug said.

Donnell approached us then, "May I have this dance with the new queen?" he said.

With a laugh, my brother said, "Of course." And off they went together. I was horrified and couldn't seem to move off the dance floor for a few minutes as I watched them dance across the room. From the sidelines I watched the crowd suspiciously, certain that someone would take offense, but no one gave them a second look. Donnell caught on to the polka steps quickly and he and Doug were talking now as they moved boisterously across the floor together.

It's Cheaper to Live in the Dark

I learned that from my second husband. We're divorced now, but I learned some things from him. He'd told me once about a book he read where a woman lived in the dark to save money. When he told me that story it seemed like a good idea. As long as he lived with me he wouldn't go along with living in the dark. Once he was gone, the first thing I did was turn out the lights. I've been married twice and divorced twice. Neither of my husbands liked my music. They didn't mind me playing it at home, but they didn't like me playing out with my band. The band wasn't all that happy with me marrying those guys. I played the accordion with one of the best of the area polka bands—The Little Polka Band. We played at festivals all around the central part of Nebraska for a long time.

I played the organ at church, too. One of my husbands didn't mind that, but one of them did. He wasn't a churchgoer and Sunday was his only day to sleep late.

He claimed my clanking around on Sunday mornings woke him up.

By the time I figured out to divorce those two husbands the band had broken up and I just never joined another one, mainly because of my legs. They had started to give out on me by then and the truth is I couldn't stand up anymore long enough to play a set. "Nobody wants to see a woman in a wheelchair playing an accordion," my mother told me. I almost believed her. And then if a few years ago I didn't see another woman in a wheelchair. She was playing the fiddle. I was glad I didn't listen to my mother that time, but I have real respect for her. She's the one who set me up so I can drive myself anywhere I want and take my chair along, and she fixed up my house so I can take care of myself. She's eighty but you'd never know it.

After I was in the wheelchair I saw my second husband once and he asked me, "You still living over there in the dark?" I told him yes I was and it was the second best thing I'd ever done, second to not being married to him anymore. He shook his head and snickered down into his beard and said "and doesn't it just beat all, the irony of your being in a wheelchair to boot." I never did understand him. "You and your literal-mindedness," he said to me that same day. "I suppose you're in that wheelchair because someone told you you couldn't walk, is that right?" He was right, but I didn't tell him that. The doctor had told me that I'd most likely lose the use of my legs eventually, and I'd taken to the wheelchair as a way to sort of save them up, so I wouldn't lose them completely.

I've been selling off some of my stuff—trying to clear out a space in a back room I have so maybe I can hire a gal to come help take care of me. I've got some nice stuff, some antiques that've been well taken care of. Yesterday I sold a doll for $350. She was worth it; I wasn't taking advantage. The woman who bought her owns an antique store. She knew what she was worth.

I sold a '64 Fender Tremolux a few months ago to a couple of young fellas who are in a band. When they plugged the thing in it made a terrible scream and then began to smoke. I knew I'd taken good care of that amplifier, always kept it covered and in a cool place. It was beyond me what had gone wrong. I figured they probably thought I was trying to take advantage of them. They conferred about it and while they were conferring I asked if they'd mind if I played the organ a little. They said they wouldn't mind if I did that. I didn't even notice them for awhile, I was so lost in my playing, but eventually I noticed those two boys had come into the room to listen to me.

"You sure can play the organ," the one with the beard said. "I've never heard anyone play the organ like that. Do you play by ear?"

"Yes I do," I said. "I taught myself. I probably don't do it right, the way you would if you'd learned it, but I can play anything if I hear it once."

Both boys shook their heads at that. "You're a genius," the tall one said. "I think you're a genius to play
like that. That was a kick hearing you play polka on the
organ." I could tell he meant it. Other than my husbands, people always did like my music.

"You ever figure out what was the problem with
that amp?" I asked them.

"It just needs a new fuse. We'll be able to fix it."

"We'd like to take it," said the one with the beard.

"That's just fine, then." They wrote a check to me
and laid it on the top of the organ.

I followed them back into the living room., "What
sort of band you boys play in?"

"We play in a rock and roll band," one of them, the
tall one, told me.

"What instrument do you play?"

"I play the electric banjo."

I'd never heard of such a thing. "You put a pick-up
in that banjo?"

"That's right. I put a pick-up in the banjo."

Now that intrigued me. I'm not much for rock 'n
roll, but I thought these were nice, polite fellows.
Mother would have liked them. I wished she were here
then. She'd have had a piece of pie to offer them. I don't
bake things like that, but my friend had brought some
plums by the day before. They were good looking fresh
plums still sitting on the counter by the sink.

"You boys like plums?"

They didn't say anything immediately, but since I

waited for an answer they finally said yes. "There's some plums there by the sink," I said. "Why don't you help yourselves to some. Wash them first." When they seemed shy I said it again. "Go on, help yourselves there."

They stayed and ate some plums. One of them, the tall one, I thought might be able to reach a box I'd been wanting down from the top of a tall dresser. He was real good about getting that when I asked him to. He complained a little about the dark, wanting to turn on the lights. When I told him about my philosophy, he said something sort of quiet about opening the shades because the sun was still free. I didn't catch it all and he didn't mean for me to, so I just ignored it like a polite person would.

Those boys asked me then about the Tremolux and that's how it came out about me playing in the polka band. They perked right up when I mentioned the accordion and asked a lot of questions. I could sort of see their minds working and wondered if they were hoping I wanted to sell the accordion too.

I was surprised then when the shorter fellow with the beard asked "Do you think you could play rock rhythms?" They were both handsome boys.

"I don't know why not," I said. "I can play most anything once I hear it." They exchanged a look. "What are you boys getting at?" I asked.

"It's just that we're playing a gig here soon and we're sort of wanting something new."

"A gig?"

"You know, a date, an engagement; we've been asked to play."

"Oh sure. I know what you mean."

"We're playing for a benefit, but most of the people who will be there have heard us a lot before, so we wanted to surprise them. It's the new thing to have unpredictable instruments—fiddles, banjos." He nodded toward his tall friend. "Whistles, you know. An accordion would be great. It'd be great to hear what an accordion would do."

"You want to play my accordion?" I asked.

He laughed. "I can't play the accordion. We wondered if you'd play with us."

That was an interesting idea. "I have to think about that," I told them; I wondered out loud how I'd practice with them.

"We'll come here if you like," the tall one said. By that time I'd thought of a few more boxes I needed brought down, so he'd been working steady while we'd had this conversation.

"Why not," I finally said. "One time can't hurt anything."

They came back the very next week—just those two. They said it was too much trouble and noise to bring the drums and the bass, but they figured if I could listen to their set I'd be able to find a place for the accordion. It turned out to be no trouble at all. The tall boy had been telling the truth about that electric banjo.

He didn't play it near right, though. He couldn't finger pick, so he wouldn't have been much good in a blue-grass band, but it sounded okay with what they were doing, some of which didn't sound like much if you ask me. Songs like one I think they called Psychotic something or other stopped and started and turned corners every which way. No sense whatsoever, but I didn't have the heart to tell those fellows they weren't particularly good musicians. My mother would have said, if she'd been around when they left, that it had sounded like two cats fighting in a tin garbage can.

It wasn't long before I had their songs figured out, though. I'm good at that, and those boys were tickled. They laughed out loud a couple of times.

"Perfect," the bearded one said. I was glad they were pleased, but I couldn't hear how it had been anywhere near perfect.

"Will you play with us next week?" that bearded boy asked.

"Why not? You fellows were so nice to come here and move those boxes down for me."

"Great. Does it work okay for us to come here to practice?"

"I don't see why not," I said. "Before you boys go, could you move that chair in the living room. It's not in a good place for me." While they were moving the chair, which also meant moving the couch and the table because they were in the way of where I wanted the chair to go, I brought up the problem of my wheelchair.

"I can stand, you know," I said. "I can, but not for long periods of time. I'd be playing the accordion in my chair here." They both seemed surprised when I said that, and at first I thought they hadn't noticed I was in a wheelchair. "I am in a wheelchair," I said. "I get around good in it, but it's there just the same."

"Sure. We know that. That's no problem," the tall fellow said. They'd tried to introduce themselves, but I can't remember names for nothing. "Boy, boy," I said then, for sure wishing I knew their names because that tall fellow was pushing the table and the lamp was threatening to fall. "Mind that lamp!" He caught it, but barely. I'd have hated to lose that lamp. My sister-in-law from my first husband gave it to me.

When the day came for the gig—I'd taken to calling it that too—I shined up my accordion and did my hair the best I could manage. I waited around most of that day and then the tall boy came. He was really handy getting me in and out of his car. It was a small car, though, and a tight squeeze with all our musical equipment in the back and my wheelchair too. He laughed once we were on the road. "We look a little like the Clampitts, don't we?"

"You interested in a job?" I asked him. "I need somebody to come and tend me and my house. I'm going to fix up that back room and you could live there."

He smiled. He had a nice smile. "I already have a job, Carol. Besides, my wife wouldn't like me moving in with another woman."

I don't know that I saw what was so funny, but I said, "You have a wife? How long you been married?"

"Four years."

"Four years? You don't look like you're out of school yet, and here you are married four years."

He laughed again. "I'm older than I look."

They hadn't mentioned we'd be playing outside. It was a windy day and they had a little trouble setting up. They were slick about it, though. I could tell they'd played a few times. They set me up front a bit apart from the drum set. The young man who drummed for them was all over those drums—sounded like a fat man falling down the stairs. I could hear that just as he warmed up. The bass player was an all right fellow, a little older than the two who'd been coming by my place. His hair was gray and he wore it long. I felt like that was an unfortunate combination, but he was nice enough. They were all nice men, even that drummer. I asked them what the name of their band was—"Bobby Steed and the Steady Boys," they said. For some reason I remember the name of the band but not the names of the band members.

"Which one of you is Bobby Steed," I asked, and they said none of them was. I was past trying to figure things out. In one of my old bands, the Bill Sibulanski Band, the leader of the band was Bill Sibulanski. I thought that was how things went.

We ran through a couple of pieces before folks started gathering on the lawn. I never heard such a four-beat racket in my life and that Bobby Steed couldn't sing his way out of a bucket. I began to feel we were making a regular spectacle of ourselves as people started filing in bringing blankets and lawn chairs—mostly young people, but a few older folks too. There were little kids everywhere and a few dogs. Before we started playing, a little wire-haired terrier kept coming close to the stage and sniffing. He was a cute little guy. Once the music started, though, he took off. I kept waiting for people to leave, but instead more came until the lawn was so full people had to stand in the back. A few came up front and danced. Others tapped their toes and bounced their heads.

The boys in the band kept smiling and nodding at me. I took that as a sign that they liked what I was doing. The music was queer but it wasn't hard—most of it a three chord progression. Shoot. I could have played those songs sleeping.

Afterward, the band helped get my accordion put away and one of them said he'd take me back home—same one as came to get me earlier. He was all wound up, which I understood from my days in the polka band. I'd come home after a dance and stay up half the night cleaning house or working on a project before I could settle down. That's what both of my husbands complained of—all my rattling around the house. I could tell this guy driving me was going to be up half the night. It's like a drug playing like that. A hyperactivity drug, and it doesn't just wear off right away. I shouldn't say that. I had a couple band members in the polka band who claimed they went right home and straight to sleep. Everyone back at that time was trying to cure me of my being wound up so my husbands would let me keep playing out.

"You want to stop by the Tam o' Shanter for a drink?" this fellow asked me. "We always go there after a gig and have a few drinks together."

"Every time, huh?"

"Yeah."

"Well then, sure." I'd used to be a drinker, but with my legs being like they are now I don't drink anymore. It seemed like a shame not to join them if it was a tradition, though. Besides, I was a little curious to hear how they felt things had gone.

The bar where we went had a low dark ceiling. Red shag carpet on the floor and half way up the walls too. It made a pretty effect. Black and red vinyl booths. Things were a little run down, but it was a sort of classy place. Our waitress was an older woman. She had a large face, square at the jaw, and frizzy strawberry-colored hair.

I was tempted to get a whiskey sour, but I decided on a 7-Up instead. The other band members were there when we arrived, and they cheered when my wheelchair came in the door. From their conversation, I figured out they had liked what I'd done. One of them said something about how the accordion threatened the vital sleaze factor. Another one disagreed and they spent a long time discussing the vital sleaze factor. I had no idea what they were talking about and pretty much drifted in and out of my own thoughts. It was nice to get out of the house for an evening. I'd enjoyed playing my accordion. I was thinking on those things when they said my name. "Carol."

"Yes," I said.

"How would you feel about a little tour?"

"A tour?"

The gray haired guy explained that they had three gigs all close together, one in Omaha, one in Council Bluffs, Iowa, and one in Maryville, Kansas. It was just a weekend—all they could do because all of them had jobs. They called it "the tri-state tour" like they thought it was funny.

"Thanks for the offer," I told them. "I think my performing days are over, though."

"Don't you miss that?" the bearded guy said.

"You bet I do. You bet I miss it," I told him. It was just a lot of work was all. And besides, I didn't say it, but I couldn't imagine playing again with these fellows, nice as they were, and even though folks came and danced and seemed to enjoy themselves, I still couldn't say I liked their music. It's a bad thing to play music you don't like. I didn't tell them all of that. They seemed happy with what they were doing. "I just can't do it," I told them that night. "I get too wound up over playing and don't get enough rest. The way I am now, I can't do that anymore like I used to when I was younger. If I was younger, maybe then I'd consider doing that tri-state tour with you. I'd be honored." And I was honored. I enjoyed those boys paying attention to me, but like my first husband always said, "attention ain't intention." I figured those boys were just talking, a little bit worked up from the gig and the alcohol, and that their tri-state tour wouldn't really happen. I don't like to waste time talking about what won't happen. I didn't say that, though. No reason to hurt their feelings.

The tall fellow lifted his glass to me. "To Carol," he said.

"Here, here," the others said and lifted their glasses to me too. Even though I was only drinking 7-Up I lifted my glass and tipped it to them.

"Well, now we know what we're looking for anyway," the gray-haired boy said. We're looking for an accordion player. Let's all keep our eyes out, and Carol, if you know of a likely candidate you'll let us know?"

"Sure," I said. "Sure I'll let you know. If you guys know of anyone interested in living in my back room, I could use some help there at home. I could use some help, you know. You'll watch out?"

They all nodded, and our glasses clinked together once again.

Hyacinths

That night long ago, before we went to sleep in the unfamiliar bed at Ben and Gemmy's house, my sister Christy and I talked about the hyacinths that had recently come up in our yard at home—grape hyacinth, their purple blossoms heavy with a sweet, fruity fragrance. We had helped our mother plant them in the fall. She loved flowers, as was clear from the daffodils, tulips, and iris that bordered our house. Mother had learned to garden from her Granny. "Granny" was one of the funny words she used. When we teased Mother about how she talked, she smiled and broke into an exaggerated version of the accent she'd been raised with. She called the people from her past hill people, as though she had come from some place far away when in fact her childhood home was only a short distance from the town of Broken Bow where we lived. Ben and Gemmy were hill people; Gemmy was mother's second cousin. We felt uncomfortable in Ben and Gemmy's house that night, and memories of hyacinths and home comforted us.

The next morning Gemmy made eggs. There was no running water in the house, only a galvanized bucket setting on the counter holding water drawn from the well. We had had to walk to an outdoor toilet that morning and the night before, like we were camping in regular life. Christy and I exchanged a glance as Gemmy drew a glass of water from the bucket on the counter. Only moments earlier one of the numerous cats prowling about the house—under the table, on the countertops, rubbing against the chairs where we sat, like moving water, liquid and constant—had lapped from the bucket. We had no appetite for the oozing eggs Gemmy set on the table. She stood back and appeared to admire us for a moment.

Ben came in from morning chores then. "Shut that door," Gemmy told him. Ben had a simple, open face. We couldn't quite figure him out. We liked him, but he seemed like a boy that might be at our school rather than a grown man, and he sounded like that now as he rushed to shut the door. "Sorry, Gemmy."

"Did you girls sleep okay?" he said eagerly as he took off his boots by the door.

"Those cats . . ." Christy started, stopping as I elbowed her roughly in the side.

"We slept fine. Thanks," I said.

"That's good to hear." Ben sat down across from us at the table and waited as Gemmy served him.

"Gemmy, you're wheezing this morning," he said as she set a plate before him. Gemmy had started breathing heavily almost as soon as Ben came in the door. Neither Christy nor I had really noticed it until then.

"It's my asthma acting up again." Her breathing became even more labored.

"Why, Gemmy, you sound plumb terrible. Did you take your medicine?" Ben pushed his chair back and went to the kitchen windowsill where a small brown prescription bottle stood. "Here now," he said as he opened it and poured a pill into his palm. "You take this now." He drew a glass of water from the bucket and watched carefully, his face mimicking Gemmy's swallowing motions as she took the pill. Once she had finished, he broke into a broad smile. "There you be."

Back at the chair, he chased a cat away from his plate and ate the cooling egg, its yolk coagulated and scabby on the plate.

"You two ready for church?" Gemmy asked us.

"Yes." We were both dressed and ready to go. "Where could we brush our teeth?" I asked.

"We'll set you up here with a bowl of water," Gemmy said.

I had pushed the egg around on my plate, hoping Gemmy wouldn't notice I hadn't eaten anything. Christy had tried the same deception.

"You girls sure don't eat much," Gemmy said. "You didn't eat a thing last night either. You feeling all right?"

"Yes, ma'am." We nodded.

"I don't know how anyone can eat so little and still stay alive. So, you're ready to go then?"

"Yes."

"Ben, you'll be ready soon?"

"I'll be ready soon as I finish eating."

"You won't neither. You're not going to church in those choring clothes."

"It'll take me no more an a minute to change."

"Don't keep us waiting," she said, and then, as though remembering something she'd forgotten, she began to breathe heavily again.

"That medicine sure isn't doing nothing for you this morning."

"No, I can tell I'm having a bad spell."

In our room while I packed our suitcase Christy mimicked Gemmy's heavy breathing. "I'm . . . having . . . a bad spell . . . Ben. I . . . don't . . . think . . . I'll make it." And then she grabbed her neck and fell on the bed in a mock swoon.

I smiled. "Get up off of there now and help me make the bed."

"Why's she do that only when he's around?"

"Who knows."

A couple of the cats had followed us into the room. They circled our suitcase on the bed. "These cats are driving me crazy." I motioned to Christy and together we pulled the bedspread back over the bed, the cats leaping to the floor as we did.

"How do they live here in the winter?" Christy whispered. "It's cold this morning, and it's spring."

I shrugged again, and Christy mimicked me. "Don't you know anything?"

"I know I'm going to kill mom for telling Gemmy it was okay for us to stay here when Gemmy asked."

"You girls coming?" Gemmy called from the next room.

"Just about." I snapped the suitcase shut.

Riding in Ben and Gemmy's big blue Buick, I watched the countryside pass by. It was May and the wildflowers were everywhere in the roadside ditches. "Did you know Gemmy has the Egyptian flu?" Ben asked us.

"Now Ben, don't be teasing those girls," Gemmy said, but she was smiling.

"What's the Egyptian flu?" Christy asked.

"She's going to be a mummy."

Both Christy and I had to think for a few seconds before looking quickly at Gemmy who smiled and nodded. Gemmy looked much too old. She was older than our mother.

"We're hoping this one will work out," Gemmy said.

"It will," Ben said. "Now don't you go talking like that. The doctor said there was no reason why . . ." They had started to talk to each other as though we weren't in the car before Ben seemed to catch himself. Outside the car window, the leafless trees and the newly planted fields, black with mud, spun by. The gravel road went up and down and around the hills like an unspooling ribbon.

"When will your baby come?" Christy asked.

"Around Thanksgiving time," Gemmy said.

"Just in time to eat a little turkey," Ben added.

"Oh, now don't go teasing again and making things up." Gemmy turned then to look at Christy. "Ben's just joking. Babies don't eat turkey."

"I know that," Christy said, obviously irritated by Gemmy's protectiveness.

Gemmy's jowly face was an ashy, green color. Her skin sagged. She wore black, cat-eye frame glasses, and her hair was wispy, balding on top. Her body seemed lumpy and formless, like a bundle of laundry pulled together by a belt. Ben, on the other hand, was tall and thin, strongly built. He had no wrinkles on his face and his skin was pink and healthy. He had an open, smiling expression, and clear, tinsel-blue eyes.

Later, at home, after Sunday dinner we scolded our mother for coercing us to go stay with Ben and Gemmy.

"It was terrible," Christy said. "Cats everywhere."

"I know," our mother said. "Ben and Gemmy always want you girls to come stay, and I figured it wouldn't hurt anything for you to go just once. They're well-meaning folks."

"Oh well," Christy went on. "They won't need us to come anymore pretty soon. They're going to have a baby of their own."

Father glanced quickly at Mother then at Christy. "Did they tell you that?"

"Yes."

Father was quiet. He seemed to be thinking, but he said nothing more about the baby.

"Well, I'll be," Mother said. She was not like the mothers of our friends. She didn't fix up, as she called it. Her hair lay flat and was cut in no particular style. She wore jeans and flannel shirts untucked. In the summer, she went barefoot or wore Birkenstock sandals. In winter, leather work boots. Our father was a district county attorney and wore suits and ties everyday. He wore a long trench coat and shiny shoes and carried a leather brief case. He smelled of spicy cologne while our mother often smelled of dirt from gardening. We had heard Father refer to himself as an elected official, and sometimes we saw signs in people's yards all around town that said, "Elect Bret Thompson." His picture appeared in the newspaper and on the large billboards on the highway. Our mother referred to the people he worked with at the county courthouse as yahoos, as in, "What are the yahoos going to do about that?" Father always laughed at her version of things. He said he relied on her down-to-earth way of seeing the world. Sometimes Christy and I thought he didn't quite understand our mother, that he took most of what she said as only humorous when we felt she often meant something serious. We had overheard her telling him once that he had sold out, that he was becoming a diehard for the status quo, and that if she'd known he'd become such a fascist, she'd never have married him.

Mother had been beautiful. Father told us that the first time he saw her she was on a horse, riding bareback, her long hair flying just like the horse's mane. He had been working on a ranch in the hills that summer, finishing his last year of college and hoping to go to law school.

"I worked on the ranch all day and went home at night and studied for the LSAT," he told us once. "I was half crazy with exhaustion the first time I saw your mother. I thought for awhile I was hallucinating, that I'd cracked up. I thought I'd seen a goddess."

Father didn't finish the story, though. He never talked about the years while he was in law school and Mother finished her degree in anthropology. He never mentioned how she hadn't wanted to move back to Broken Bow, how to her the town seemed to be stuck in time—how she felt they justified themselves for their lack of progress with what she called nostalgic self-congratulation. She thought the town was fossilized in the past, and rather than seeing it as quaint or wholesome the way Father did, she saw it as stubborn and ignorant. These were things we put together over time. Christy and I saw early on that the stories our parents told were never the same. Mother said they'd moved back against her will because of my father's political aspirations. She always emphasized the word ass in aspirations.

In church the next Sunday Ben was alone. Gemmy was in the hospital, we figured because of her asthma. I watched Ben during the services. He wore the same ugly dark blue suit he wore each week. Without Gemmy he seemed sad, and I couldn't quite understand how they got along or why Ben was happier with Gemmy. Gemmy was old, not pretty. She was grumpy and always sick.

"Why did Ben marry Gemmy?" I asked Mother afterwards, half expecting her to scold me for the question, but she laughed instead.

"You've been watching, haven't you?"

"I guess."

"Then you've probably noticed some things about Ben."

"He's not like other grownups."

"That's right. He and Gemmy take care of one another."

"How does he take care of Gemmy?"

Mother hesitated. "Gemmy isn't like Ben. She's smart enough, but she's got some problems."

"Like being sick all the time?"

"That's part of it. She's . . . she gets sad sometimes and Ben has to remind her to take her medicine, and he reminds her how to be happy."

"Father doesn't think they should have a baby, does he?"

A dark look crossed Mother's face. "I don't know exactly what he's thinking these days."

"Why don't people think Ben and Gemmy should have the baby?"

"I think I've answered enough questions for now."

Mother had told us stories about her fierce Granny, and I had to think of her Granny now as I watched my mother's jaw set. After her Granny was widowed, she raised seven children without any help. It made her a harsh woman, no frills, but Mother had understood this ferocious little Granny, only 4′8″ tall, and as a child had worked beside her in the garden. As they dug and planted together, she said, her Granny's face softened, her frown faded, and in the garden, she became a different person. She told Mother stories about how when her husband died, the area ranchers tried to take her land away. They had said it was to protect her, that she couldn't raise both cattle and a houseful of kids, but she had known they only wanted her land for themselves. She had stood up to them and raised her seven children to be loyal to what they believed. No one ever took anything away from her.

Mother had now and then mentioned how it was a good thing that her Granny had not lived to see her marry a town boy. She was only half joking when she said her Granny most likely would have come and switched her all the way back home where she belonged.

As Gemmy's pregnancy became more obvious through that summer I saw that most of the adults we knew were worried about it. Ben seemed to be trying to make everyone feel better, reassuring them. I didn't hear any of what he said, but I saw him talking to people after church each Sunday with an earnest, pleading expression on his face.

Gemmy had always seemed like an outsider with the women, and, unlike Ben, didn't appear to make any effort now to reassure or explain to people. She kept herself apart more than usual, seemed distant, closed off. Ben tried to include her, but Gemmy didn't respond. I had the feeling she was talking to her baby—turned inward. Through that summer and fall there were several hospitalizations.

"Is it Gemmy's asthma again?" Christy asked.

Father hesitated. "Not exactly asthma." He hesitated again. "Just some problems."

"Nothing's wrong with the baby, is it?" she said.

"No, as far as I know the baby's fine." Father seemed sad and preoccupied when he said that.

Afterward, in our bedroom Christy continued to babble about the baby. She loved babies. "I can't wait to see the baby. If it's a girl, I hope they name her Star."

"You are such an idiot," I said.

"Why am I an idiot?"

"I don't know why. You just are. Always going on about that baby. Can't you see nobody wants to talk about it? It'll probably be a little freak of nature and nobody wants it to be born."

"I want it to be born. Gemmy and Ben want it to be born," she said. "It won't be a freak of nature. I pray for the baby every night. Ben asked me to. And Ben and Gemmy are praying every night too."

I rolled my eyes. "So what if you're right. Would you want to be a baby living in that house with them?"

Christy hesitated. She was quiet for a long time. Our window was open and the curtains filled with the breeze, fluttered, and then sucked back against the screen. Christy watched the movement of the curtains, and as she watched, her face began to change. She seemed to have seen something frightening, and her face fell suddenly as she looked at me. "The poor baby," she said. She looked so crestfallen that I tried to make up for what I had said earlier.

"Oh, it'll probably be okay. The baby won't know any different. They'll fix things up."

Tears coursed down Christy's face. "No, they won't. The poor baby. It'll be so afraid. It'll have to eat terrible food and the cats will be everywhere . . . in its crib." More tears.

I tried to think of a way to reassure my sister. "They'll make the cats stay outside. Once the baby is here. And Gemmy will learn to cook better. She will. It'll be okay."

Christy looked at me through tear-filled eyes. "Do you really think so?"

"Things will be okay."

She studied me for awhile. "No, they won't," she said finally. "They won't be okay." Her voice sounded strangely adult, resigned. I felt bad for having taken away her dream of the baby, and I knew that now Christy's fears would manifest themselves in nightmares and anxious questions.

Sure enough, at dinner that night. "What will happen to the baby?"

"What do you mean?" Father asked.

"How will the baby live with Gemmy and Ben at that house?"

Father cleared his throat. "I'm not sure, but the first thing they need to do is get married," he said. I was surprised to learn they weren't married. "We've talked to them about how they need to get straight with God first."

"That's nonsense," my mother said. "What possible business is it of yours?" My father didn't answer her, and she went on. "What is happening to you?" she said. I thought she was referring to the men's group at church. Around the first time we heard about Gemmy's baby, the men's group Father was involved with at church had started meeting two nights a week instead of one.

"So, you're getting together again to talk about how to be good family men, huh?" My mother liked to say when he was leaving.

"I'll be home by 10:00," Father always said without acknowledging my mother's point.

The men's group had started to make regular presentations on Sunday mornings in church. They said church members needed to become concerned citizens, to be registered voters, to start supporting the things they believed in, to help change our corrupt government. I didn't pay much attention to these talks, but I always noticed my mother's response, a slight stiffening as she crossed her arms and pressed her mouth tightly closed.

My father ignored my mother that night as though ignoring a child having a tantrum. I had never seen him act that way and Mother seemed slightly confused too. "Some people in town have tried to go out and help them get ready for the baby," he said to Christy and me. "The men's group offered to put in indoor plumbing for them, but they wouldn't hear of it."

"Why not?" I asked.

"Because they like things the way they are," Mother interrupted. "They're used to it, and goodness knows," Mother's voice took on a peculiar tone like she was arguing with someone instead of just talking to us. "People used to live like that all the time and not all that long ago. There was no running water on the ranch when I was growing up until I was in high school. And all around the world now there are people with less, and still the human race continues. You'd think in this country it was a crime to be poor."

We were surprised when a strange thing happened then, something neither Christy nor I had ever seen. Mother began to cry. It was as though we were no longer there as Father said, "Now Jeannie, no one's saying it's a crime. What's the matter here?"

"They'll try to take that baby away from Gemmy. And half of it'll be just because they aren't married, and their house isn't modern. They'll use the excuse that Gemmy's mentally ill and Benny's slow, but really it will just be because they don't try to live like middle-class drudges and dupes."

When she said that, Father's mouth set in a straight line. He patted Mother's shoulder without looking at her. "You're getting yourself worked up, Jeannie." I was surprised that Father wouldn't know that was the wrong thing to say.

Mother's eyes flashed, "Oh am I?" I saw in that moment what my Father must have seen that day he first came upon her in the hills, that half-wild, fierce creature.

Father went on patting her shoulder, unaware, it seemed, of her rage. "We'll have to see how things go," he was saying. "We probably won't have to intervene."

"I know you won't," she said, and shrugged his hand away. "I won't let you. I won't allow it to happen. I'm not going to sit by and watch that happen. I know how people think around here, though, and I can see already by their meddlesomeness what they're wanting to do. I don't blame Ben and Gemmy for not allowing them in their house. I don't blame them. They should stand up for themselves."

"The girls," Father said then, though I felt he was not trying to protect us so much as change the subject.

Timothy was born as Ben had predicted the week before Thanksgiving, and to all of our surprise the birth was uncomplicated. The next week they came to church even though it had snowed the night before. That day I heard the murmuring Mother had predicted. "What were they thinking? Driving on those roads with that baby? What would have happened if they'd gotten stuck? Or run into a ditch?"

I was certain Ben and Gemmy must have heard the criticism, too, but Gemmy seemed calm. She showed the baby to those who asked to see and otherwise seemed quiet and confident as though she knew what she was doing. Ben was beside himself, beaming and giddy and not at all helpful, but Gemmy didn't seem to mind.

The baby himself was a shock. His face was thin and odd. It seemed to have been made of clay—pinched into shape by a kindergartner's hand. He looked more like a little hairless animal or a sick old man than a newborn. He had Gemmy's same greenish colored skin.

Mother tried to reassure us. "He's just tiny is all. He's a small newborn and they sometimes look that way."

In the weeks to come two things happened: the baby never did change for the better—by then we had heard the words "failure to thrive"—and the community didn't attempt to take the baby away as Mother had feared. But Mother seemed to have geared up for a fight anyway. It seemed only Christy and I saw in those weeks before Timothy was born the degree to which she was prepared to do battle. She cleaned the house from top to bottom, washing walls and windows, polishing woodwork, pulling everything from closets and cupboards, sorting, throwing, and organizing, muttering under her breath all the while. Meals were simple and slightly bizarre, like an afterthought: broccoli and biscuits, or one time only frozen peas, thawed, not cooked. Our house was in disruption and when Christy and I came home from school we were never certain what we would find. We didn't know where our calm, cheerful mother had gone or how she had been replaced by this agent for order.

Not long after Timothy was born, one Sunday morning, Mother, still wearing her flannel pajamas at the kitchen table, said to Father, "You're on your own for church this morning. The girls and I won't be going with you."

Father looked up from the paper. Behind his glasses his eyes were slightly unfocused. "Are you sick?"

Mother shrugged. Christy and I exchanged a glance. We were not disappointed to be staying home. "We're just not going." Father didn't say anything as he went back to reading the paper, and I noticed he didn't say goodbye when he left an hour later, Mother still at the table in her pajamas reading a magazine.

Mother had never been one to like church or other community events, often telling us before we went to church not to let any of their silly notions get to us. "It's just people talking, not God speaking like they want you to believe." We always understood we did certain things for the sake of Father's job, but we were bewildered when in the weeks to come she still refused to go to church. Because of that, we only saw baby Timothy if we happened to see Ben and Gemmy at the grocery store. We had a sense that some people felt sorry for Mother, but that most of them were put out with her. One time when we saw Mrs. Henfield at the grocery store and she told Mother she was praying for her, Mother answered, "Why don't you pray for yourself instead?" I was embarrassed for Mother and didn't want to look at Mrs. Henfield. When I finally did look up, Mrs. Henfield had a little smile on her face, like she wasn't offended at all.

Later, when we got in the car, Mother slammed the door. "We're going to start shopping in Lexington. I don't want to see any of these people. Not anyone. I'm so sick of this town and these self-righteous idiots I could puke." Christy and I wanted to laugh because Mother had said the word puke, but we didn't. She wasn't being funny anymore like she used to be. She had seen something new in the town perhaps, something menacing and powerful and dangerous while Gemmy was pregnant.

Although Christy and I had separate bedrooms, we started sleeping together during that time and we often talked at night.

"She won't go away, will she?" Christy said one night.

"No," I said, though the same fear had crossed my mind.

"Do you think they'll get a divorce?"

"No," I said again, though I had feared that, too. I didn't know what parents could or couldn't do, but I had decided to protect Christy. She sighed as though relieved and curled onto her side like a little leaf closing for the night, and I snuggled against her back.

At first Father acted like nothing was wrong. He came home and cheerfully greeted all of us, ignoring Mother's silences and eating the strange meals without comment. We had hoped for some clue from him about what was happening, and what we saw instead was how confused and afraid he was. Mother seemed to have disengaged from her normal day-to-day life. I couldn't say what had made her change, but at night when we talked, Christy and I decided our mother had become willing to sacrifice everything, her friendships, her marriage, maybe even us, for the sake of the fight. We knew it was some idea she had in mind, some noble purpose. If baby Timothy failed to thrive, and he never did become the pink-cheeked baby we had hoped he would, Father and everyone else in town seemed to feel Mother was thriving wrongly. From somewhere we couldn't see, her beliefs swelled inside her, and she seemed both more confident and less content. Mother had moved beyond all of us.

Eventually, it seemed as though only Christy and I could see what would happen. We could see Mother's double, her future self, standing there beside her while her old self struggled to give birth to the new. The adults seemed to lack our second sight, for if they could have seen the other, the future woman, they would not have wasted their time fighting to save the old one. All the community knew was that Mother had ceased to be predictable, had ceased to play the role we had all come to depend on. She had jumped the track, while the people around her had remained the same. She knew them, but they did not know her.

What Christy and I saw that others, even Father, couldn't seem to see was why Gemmy's pregnancy had been the catalyst for this change. We knew Mother's stories, after all, and Christy and I believed that what she was doing had been there in her nature all along and was bound to happen. She had learned it while planting bulbs with her Granny. We decided that if it hadn't been Gemmy's baby it would have been something else, a local ordinance, a church doctrine, a practice at the school. Her rebellion had lain dormant, and, like a hyacinth bulb, when the time was right her true self emerged. We both understood and feared what she would do next, for we had seen already in the stories of her Granny a glimpse of the fierce and wonderful woman she would become.

The Girls

Becca liked dogs. She might even have called herself a dog person, but she couldn't quite figure out why Professor Blakely had asked her to watch his dogs while he was in Italy for a conference during the week of fall break. Only later did she realize she hadn't been his first choice. Of course not. What had she been thinking? Everyone on the small campus of Pilgrim's College knew how much Professor Blakely loved his dogs. They were his children. Some of the guys in the fraternities liked to joke that they were more than his children. Professor Blakely was so closely associated with his dogs that he was known around campus, when the students talked among themselves, as Dog-boy.

As the dog-sitting gig got closer, Becca heard from others who had done it before. "Wow. You sure you want to do that?" a guy in her Advanced Theater Design class asked. "You'll be cooped up in that house, and . . ." He didn't go on. It was like this with everyone, a strange reticence just at the moment they were about to give her details. When she pressed for more, they all shrugged. "You'll see," was the reply. All Becca knew was that she needed a letter of recommendation from Professor Blakely if she wanted to get into graduate school.

Becca went to Professor Blakely's house on the Thursday before he was scheduled to leave to "meet the girls," as he called them. From the first moment she saw them, Becca was put off by the dogs' behavior. A large boxer named Desdemona, and a pug named Hetta. They seemed more like naughty children than the well-trained animals she had expected of a true dog lover. When she had first entered the house, the pug barked wildly and the boxer sniffed at her crotch and then, having apparently found Becca acceptable, jumped up, her large paws resting on Becca's shoulders.

Becca was put off by the house as well. There was a weird violence at work in most of the rooms—both in color and in choice of decor. The closer she looked the more troubled Becca felt. If the images weren't violent they were pornographic, shocking. She surreptitiously looked closer at several small prints in the den only to find they were a black and white series of beautifully framed, vulgar postcards—not anything like the burlesque, titillating, slightly humorous postcards she had found in her grandfather's desk the summer she was ten, but explicit photographs of what seemed like every sort of sexual activity possible. She turned away, flushed and disoriented, afraid Blakely had noticed her discomfort. He didn't seem to as he moved about the room in a businesslike manner, explaining that she must make herself at home. He acted as though there was nothing strange about the fact that a large, erect, stone penis served as a paper weight on the desk next to the phone.

Blakely invited Becca to stay for tea after he'd shown her around the house. He talked as he set the kettle on to boil, a complicated explanation of both dogs' personalities and preferences. He set a plate in the middle of the table. "Would you mind putting out the cookies?" he asked and handed her three boxes.

"Hetta is very intelligent," Blakely said as he filled a tea ball. "She's affectionate but not above withholding affection for her own manipulative purposes." He looked down at Hetta who stood at his feet watching him. "Isn't that right, you little vamp, you?" Hetta opened her mouth and sneezed loudly. Blakely laughed. He looked at Becca. "She's such an actress."

While Blakely tended the teapot, Becca looked more closely at the kitchen. Like the rest of the house it was eccentric, crowded with things. A riot of colors—tangerine seeming to dominate—the kitchen was filled with the same violent details found in the rest of the house. From the little pewter pistols that served as handles and the machete-like hinges on the cabinet doors, to the serving dish on which she was now placing the cookies—a large open mouth, like a close-up of a vintage Hollywood scream. Teeth lined the top and bottom edges while the center of the plate featured a ridged palate and a slimy looking tongue.

Blakely poured tea into cups shaped like fish, the open mouth forming the mouth of the cup. He gestured for her to sit down across from him. Suddenly, sitting across from Blakely, Becca panicked at the need to carry her end of the conversation. She was not someone who felt comfortable hanging out and chatting with her professors, and Blakely was more imposing than most. He wore his white hair cut short. It was always the same length, which led Becca to believe he had it barbered every week. Although he wore the customary uniform of the Humanities professor—corduroy trousers and tweed jackets, wool vests and cotton or linen shirts—he did not go for the common rumpled, just-slept-in look. He was immaculate. His clothes were pressed, his shoes shone, his skin and teeth gleamed. Even with all of its eccentricities, the house too was spotless. She had noticed this especially in the only room where there were no violent or pornographic images. In the back of the house, overlooking the backyard flower garden, the room had contained nothing but a white carpet which matched the white walls and ceiling. Recessed lights shone on the only object—a white orchid in bloom, in a blue ceramic pot. Becca knew it was an orchid only because Professor Blakely had told her when he gave her detailed watering instructions—only once while he was away and then only watered from the bottom. If the plant looked strange for any reason she was to call immediately a man named Vic Epperly. Under no circumstances was she to touch the plant. Already Becca had a reverent feeling toward the orchid. It was a rare variety, Blakely had told her, given to him by a grower in Florida. There were only a handful of this particular species left in the world.

Almost as soon as Blakely had sat down at the table, inviting Becca to help herself to the cookies, he said, "Treats," and the dogs bounded up from where they had been resting near the cabinets. It was clear Hetta was the leader. She was the first up to the table, leaping into the chair to the right of Blakely. Without interference from him, she proceeded to remove a cookie from the mouth plate with her teeth. Becca drew back in surprise and felt herself cringe involuntarily, awaiting the inevitable irate response from Blakely. Instead Blakely laughed and patted the dog's head.

"Hetta want some tea with the big people?"

Hetta wagged her curled tail and seemed to grin and nod. Blakely was delighted. At the same time Hetta was being indulged, Desdemona stood up on her hind legs and placed her large paws on the table. She, too, stuck her enormous head over the plate of cookies and snatched one with her teeth—rather daintily for a large dog.

No way, Becca thought. No way does he let her get away with that. But Blakely laughed again. "Mona, you beautiful thing, you. Are you starving? Are you starving, girl?" Desdemona also seemed to smile at Blakely as she swallowed the cookie in one big gulp.

"I allow the girls one treat each day," Blakely said to Becca, smiling in satisfaction. "Only one. Anything they want."

As he let Becca out the door a little later, Blakely gave her a spare key. "I'll leave the important numbers for you—the vet, the plumber, Vic. My friend Alan can be available in a pinch. I'll leave his number, too. My one request is that you please not leave the girls alone overnight. They're quite terrified to be by themselves at night. It's why I have someone sit with them."

"Okay," Becca said.

"So you'll be here early Saturday morning?" he went on. "Eight o'clock? I'll want to know you're here with the girls before I leave for the airport."

"All right," Becca said. Hetta and Desdemona crowded around Blakely's legs as Becca opened the door to go.

"Say goodbye to Becca," Blakely instructed the dogs. While she walked toward her car, Becca heard both dogs yip and howl. When she turned around to look, Blakely was laughing, his head thrown back just like the dogs' heads. She waved, though she wasn't sure any of them noticed.

On Saturday, after Professor Blakely left, Becca was alone with the girls. The "goyles," as she'd taken to calling them to herself. The dogs were silent and wary in Blakely's absence. They seemed depressed, and slept together much of the day, Hetta curled between

Desdemona's front paws. When they weren't sleeping they skulked along the walls. On a couple of occasions when Becca got up to get a drink from the kitchen or go to the bathroom, she startled the dogs from where it seemed they had been spying on her. When she surprised them like that there was a frantic scrabbling of claws on the wood floors—large claws and little claws—as they made their escape from her. Silly goyles.

That afternoon Leslie Ann came by to "check out the digs." She talked like that.

Leslie Ann snooped through every room responding out loud as Becca had silently before. By now Becca had taken more detailed note of the strangeness of the house and she showed the most startling things to Leslie Ann as they went through every room. On two whole shelves in the library were books about the history of torture. In the downstairs bathroom, the strange instruments hanging on the wall Becca now knew were torture devices. She'd seen them in some of the books. There was a large collection of books on human sacrifice, a series on mass murderers, and an even larger collection of pornography.

Leslie Ann giggled. "Oh no. He's such a pervert. Didn't you always know it? Everyone says he's a pervert—a closet pervert, you know. That's the worst kind."

"Is there a good kind of pervert?" Becca said.

"You know what I mean. There's the kind of pervert that you know is a pervert, so you can be prepared. You stay away from them. But the closet pervert, you never know what they'll do. Those are the serial killers and the pedophiles."

"You've thought about this a lot, haven't you?"

"Haven't you?"

"Not really," Becca said.

"He's a freak," Leslie Ann said. "This place is freaky. Aren't you going to be afraid to stay here alone at night?"

"I'll be all right," Becca said, though she had to admit she was a little jittery around all of the masks—horrific things, more like death masks than anything else she could describe. They had been arranged in such a way that she caught sight of them when coming around a corner or in the reflection of a mirror. Still, Becca felt she had to put on a brave front for Leslie Ann.

"What's this about?" Leslie Ann said when she discovered the white room.

"It's the orchid's room," Becca said. Already Becca had begun to think it was normal that a plant should have its own space.

Leslie Ann looked at Becca with a puzzled expression but didn't say anything as she looked back into the room again. Then turning to Becca, she said, "Don't you just want to have sex on that carpet?"

"No," Becca said, hoping she didn't sound as shocked as she felt.

"You're kidding. You didn't think about having sex on it?"

"No. It's the last thing I thought about doing."

Leslie Ann appeared slightly put out with her. "What's wrong with you?"

"What's wrong with me? What's wrong with you? You and your elaborate theories about perversion."

They left their argument as they moved to the upstairs where there were more marvels. Behind them the dogs crept like shadows . . . freezing in a crouch if Leslie Ann and Becca stopped and looked at them. Leslie Ann thought it was hilarious and deliberately stopped and turned a number of times. "Quit tweaking their wee brains," Becca said, but Leslie Ann was having too much fun. Finally, she turned once and ran toward them with a fierce cry. The dogs yelped and clattered down the stairs.

"Those are mutant dogs," she informed Becca. "They aren't normal."

When Leslie Ann left, Becca fed both dogs. They seemed to warm to her after that, creeping up to sit beside her where she had sprawled on the living room rug to watch TV.

"Hey, goyles," she said and reached to stroke their heads. Hetta initially pulled away, but then leaned into the caress. Eventually, her snubbed nose wheezed into Becca's face. Desdemona responded immediately, her perky ears moving even farther forward than usual. She studied Becca closely, and finally licked her hand.

"You rascals," Becca said. "You want a treat?" At the

word, they were off, racing for the kitchen. Desdemona leading while Hetta's little legs tried to catch up.

"Won't it be strange if you aren't there? It's your birthday party after all," Leslie Ann was saying on the phone. She had arranged a party in Omaha with some friends from the university theater department that happened to coincide with Becca's birthday. "Your twenty-first birthday party," she added as though that would make their discussion more meaningful.

"It's hardly my birthday party, Leslie Ann."

"It won't be as much fun without you," Leslie Ann said.

Becca felt irritated by the exaggeration. "I'm sure the party will be a great success even without me."

"Don't be sarcastic."

"I can't go, Leslie Ann. I have to be here with the girls. I can't be out late like that."

"Those dogs will be fine for one night. Besides, honestly, we'll get you home. Chad and I will personally ensure you'll be home by midnight at the latest. We'll leave early."

"No you won't. You won't. You're kidding yourself but you're not kidding me."

"My, aren't we little Miss Rejoinder today," Leslie Ann said. "I'm not going to quit bugging you, you know. I'm not going to quit until you give in."

Becca had been in this predicament with Leslie Ann

more times than she wanted to remember. Leslie Ann's powers of pestering were legendary. Becca both liked and detested Leslie Ann.

"Those damn dogs will be okay. They're dogs, not children."

"To Blakely they're children. I promised him I wouldn't stay away overnight."

"Grow up, will you?" Leslie Ann was using her put out voice again. "We'll be there at six on Friday to get you. I told you we'd get you home. Remember to wear a Halloween costume. Oh, yeah, Chad's bringing a friend."

Becca sighed. "Don't bring anyone on my account, please."

"Oh, no problem," Leslie Ann said brightly, realizing she had won the argument. "His friend Stephen is in town, high school buddy. You'll like him. He's a riot."

"Oh great, a riot." When Becca hung up the phone she realized she didn't feel as bad about going as she thought she would. She felt the teeniest bit excited having something to look forward to for the weekend. Maybe Leslie Ann knew her better than she knew herself. Maybe she was one of those women who said no and really meant yes.

When Becca woke up the following morning, Hetta and Desdemona acted as though she had always been there. They no longer sulked around the house. They knew who was feeding them now. That was good. Becca felt better, too, not having to deal with their depression.

That morning Professor Blakely called. He had set his alarm in Milan for some absurd time of the night, so he could call at exactly 9:00 a.m. Checking up on her, Becca figured, making sure she was there in the morning.

"How is everything?" he said.

"Things are fine." Becca didn't elaborate.

"The dogs are okay?" He sounded a little frightened by her reticence.

"Oh sure, the dogs are great. They're great," Becca said. "Hetta is standing here at my feet watching me talk to you, and Desdemona is by the sink. I think she's wanting more water."

"I'll wait while you get it for her," Blakely said, sounding happier now that she'd given him a few details.

Becca carried the phone to the sink and filled Desdemona's bowl. "Okay, that's done," she said. "She's drinking now, can you hear?" She held the phone away from her slightly.

"No, I can't hear it." Blakely sounded disappointed. "I can just see her, though. Is she looking up and smiling at you?"

She wasn't, but Becca said, "Yes, now that you say it, she is."

Blakely laughed again. "The orchid's okay?"

"Perfect. I haven't touched it. I'll water it day after tomorrow."

"Great. I'm so glad you remembered."

"How's the conference?" Becca said, not knowing how one talked to professors about things like conferences. She wasn't even certain what Blakely was doing there. He hadn't mentioned it.

"Splendid," he said. "It's always lovely to get together with a bunch of people who despise one another's research and loathe one another's opinions. We're having a lovely brawl after each session. Very invigorating. We'll all leave battered and better off for it."

Becca didn't know if he was serious or sarcastic. "That's nice," she said.

Blakely laughed again. "That's one way of putting it. I must try to sleep through what is left of this night. Hugs and kisses to the girls from me."

"Sure," Becca said looking dubiously at Hetta and Desdemona. Hugs and kisses? Not likely. After she hung up she said. "The big guy called. He says hi and hugs and kisses." Both of the dogs looked up at her. "What are you looking at me for? What am I supposed to do? Entertain you, too?" Becca thought for a while. "Do you want to go for a walk?" At the word "walk" both dogs grew animated. They ran back and forth between her and the door, barking, until she'd managed to find and hook onto their collars both of their leashes. Once the door was opened Desdemona was off in a bounding rush, Hetta scampering and wheezing in her wake. "Wait up, Desi," Becca said. The dog flung herself to the end of her leash and strained, then bounded back to Becca.

Fallen leaves scuttled along on the streets and sidewalks. A gusty wind blew the balmy air. Many of the front porches in the neighborhood sported jack-o'-lanterns carved for Halloween. She'd have to come up with a costume for the party this weekend. Having a birthday on the 31st of October meant she'd spent more than her share of birthdays disguised as a witch or a ghost. She wasn't optimistic about her ability to be any more creative this year, not with the dogs.

That night Becca allowed both dogs to sleep on the bed with her. She woke in the morning slightly disoriented and was greeted with Hetta's nose in her face.

"Hetta, someone could die from your breath." Hetta seemed to laugh at the prospect. Desdemona stirred at the bottom of the bed. The paper was there on the stoop as she let the dogs out. A newspaper, a house, two dogs. She was almost a real adult human being. It seemed strange and nice. She made a pot of coffee, filled the dog's bowls and let them back in. The sun streamed into the kitchen through the large back windows. In only a few days, Becca had become accustomed to the weirdness of the house. The violent decor no longer bothered her. It was just there, a subtext to everything, like a scream in another room at the doctor's office, slightly startling but not entirely out of the question.

Later, Becca stood to clear the table. As she moved to fold the newspaper, the gesture caused an odd reaction in the dogs. Both of them stood up and tensed. She rattled the paper and they tensed further as though they were about to bolt. Becca shook her head, smiled quizzically. When she shook the paper once again they were off, running insanely through the house. She was flabbergasted. The dogs returned to the kitchen then, hesitant, clearly waiting for her. Becca picked up the paper and noticed the dogs go tense again. She shook it and they were off once more. This time she understood it was a game and she dropped the paper and chased them. Desdemona clattered across the wood floors, her nails sounding like cups breaking, her long muscular legs loping, bumping into doorways. Hetta skittered and slid along the slick floors, sometimes sliding on her hind end. They huffed and panted and ran through the house with Becca chasing after. This went on for several minutes and then suddenly both Hetta and Desdemona, as if on cue, turned and began to chase her. Becca, though startled, ran. She giggled with the sheer joy of the chase, shrieking as she came to tight corners where she felt them bearing down on her. The dogs followed madly. They played this game far longer than Becca would have wanted to admit to anyone she knew. She was amazed, when at last all of them landed together on the living room rug where they panted in silence for awhile, to find that they had been playing together for over an hour. "You squirrelly beasts, you.

Does Professor Blakely play that game with you every morning?" Becca smiled to think of Professor Blakely chasing and being chased through the house every morning before going to class.

When all of them were rested, they went for a walk. Becca had figured out how to keep Desdemona in a little better check with the leash so that she wasn't forever being pulled between the two dogs. It was almost noon by the time they returned to the house, and Becca wondered where the time had gone. She hadn't once felt as though she wanted to see anyone.

In the late afternoon, as the sun began to set, the house felt cozy and warm. The dogs were napping and Becca wandered toward the orchid room to check on the orchid. In the dying sun, the flower seemed to radiate. It was an amazing sight, and Becca sat cross legged on the floor outside the room just to watch. Later, when she realized the house was very dark, she couldn't account for how the time had passed or what she had done in the duration. Her legs were stiff from sitting so long in one position. Becca felt slightly disoriented as she stood to feed the dogs. Both of them looked up from naps as she turned on the lights in the living room.

Remembering she hadn't given the dogs their treat that day, Becca cut up some cheese and crackers to set on the table. They sat together at the table, Hetta in one chair, Becca in another, and Desdemona standing on her back legs, like three friends, two with really bad manners. It was a trick, Becca realized, something that

Blakely had taught them to do. And Becca saw the humor of it as she sat there with them.

Professor Blakely called again the next morning just as she was getting ready to take the dogs for a walk. They were leashed and ready to go, waiting with their faces toward the door as she ran for the phone.

"We're fine," she said in response to his query. "I was just getting ready to take them on a walk. They're standing by the door waiting right now. They keep looking back toward me and wondering why we aren't going."

"Terrific. So you're walking them, then?"

"Twice a day."

"Terrific. That's terrific. That puts my mind at ease. Did you water the orchid then, too?"

"Not yet. It was next on my schedule when we got back from the walk." Becca knew without him saying it that Blakely would worry all day if he thought the orchid might not get watered. "Would you like to wait while I do that right now?"

"Yes. Don't worry about the time. These calls are costing me a fortune. It's no problem. It'll be worth the peace of mind knowing everything's okay. Don't hurry through it, though, take your time and do it right. You remember how I showed you?"

"Yes. I'll be right back." Becca filled the pitcher, kicked her shoes off and entered the white room. As she walked in, she felt as though she were intruding in some way. She slowly watered from the bottom, careful not to spill any water on the rug. When the job was finished, she came back on the phone. "All finished."

"Excellent," she heard from the other end of the line. "I won't keep the girls waiting much longer for their walk. I know how they are." In fact, while he was holding, Desdemona had barked a couple of times and Hetta had yipped impatiently. "Could you, though, before I hang up put the phone to Hetta's ear, please," Blakely said.

"Sure." Becca knelt and called to Hetta, who walked hesitantly toward her. "Here, Hetta. Listen."

From the distance, Becca could hear Blakely's voice through the phone lines. "Hettie. Sweetie, it's Daddy."

Hetta whimpered and looked at Becca, who patted her head. She barked then and Becca heard Blakely's tinny laugh across the phone. He was still laughing as Becca put the phone back to her ear. When he grew quiet, Becca said. "Did you want to talk to Desdemona, too?"

"I've got to go now," he said. "Next time, though. What did Hettie do when she heard my voice?"

"She looked confused."

"Oh," Blakely said. Becca knew she should elaborate, describe how cute Hetta had been as she looked around the kitchen for Blakely, but the moment seemed to have passed before Becca could find the words, and then he was hanging up the phone.

That afternoon Leslie Ann called. "You ready for the party?"

157

"As ready as I'll ever be," Becca said, sounding grumpier than she felt.

"What are you wearing?"

"I haven't had time to think about that."

"Haven't had time? You have nothing but time. What's the matter with you?"

"It just isn't a priority," Becca said.

"Well, since you're Miss Dog-person right now why not go as Cruella De Vil?" Leslie Ann ventured. "We could rummage through the wardrobe room at Master's Hall and find a fur coat and some weird costume jewelry, a cigarette holder. Doesn't that sound good to you?"

"It sounds fine," Becca said, knowing the effect her lack of enthusiasm would have on Leslie Ann.

Leslie Ann brooded. "You're such a wet blanket, Becca. I'm trying to help you here."

"Sure. I see that. Sorry. Let's plan to meet this afternoon and put together a costume. It'd do me good to get out of here for a while anyway."

"That's more like it," Leslie Ann said. "I'll get a key from Dr. Williamson, and meet you there at two."

Although Becca was a little early for the meeting later that afternoon, Leslie Ann had already arrived. The door was ajar, wedged by a rock. Inside, only the hall light was on, the building a little eerie and cold. Like all campus buildings when they weren't lit and filled with students, it felt unfamiliar now.

Leslie Ann was in the wardrobe room sorting through the racks of clothes. She looked up as Becca entered the room. "Hey," she said. "I've found some coats and I'm looking now for a dress. Why don't you look through the props for a cigarette holder?"

Becca held up a couple of the coats and turned slightly in the full length mirrors.

"Any of those going to work?" Leslie Ann said, glancing up.

"There seem to be some possibilities." Becca left the coats and went to the boxes of props stacked by category on large metal shelves. She knew the inventory fairly well after working on production for over three years, and quickly came to a box that seemed promising. With a slight groan, she pulled it from the shelf.

"How are you getting along over at Blakely's? Are those dogs driving you crazy yet? They drive everyone crazy. Anyone who's ever watched them for him. He doesn't leave much anymore because of it."

"I'm doing all right," Becca said.

Once they had put together a costume for Becca, Leslie Ann made suggestions for makeup and hair. Leslie Ann looked at Becca calculatingly. "It's probably a good thing you never considered being an actress," she said.

"What's that supposed to mean?"

Leslie Ann shrugged. "You've got the looks, the height, but you don't seem to have the passion to make a character come alive. Somehow even in a great costume, you don't seem to have what it takes to be Cruella," she said as though Becca should ashamed of herself.

Before Leslie Ann and the guys came by the evening of the party, Becca had a talk with the girls. She carefully put out more than enough food to get them through the evening and made sure the dog door worked if they needed to go out. Becca explained she was leaving and that she'd be back that night, but that it might be late. As she was talking both of them watched her intently and she never once doubted they were on some level understanding what she was saying. "Use the doggy door if you need to go out, you hear that, Desdemona?" she said since Desdemona was younger and didn't always seem as bright as Hetta. Desdemona licked Becca's hand like maybe she thought she was being scolded and wanted to appease her. Becca patted her head. "You'll be good, won't you? You okay, Hetta?" Hetta looked at Becca with her runny eyes. Becca wouldn't get off quite so easily with her.

The dogs stayed close while Becca transformed herself into Cruella De Vil. They seemed to sense something was happening. They watched as she teased up her hair and streaked the front, put on the jewelry Leslie Ann had found, and then applied more makeup than ten women should wear.

Later, the dogs hid away when Leslie Ann and the guys arrived. Almost as soon as they walked into the house, Leslie Ann made Becca turn around in her costume. "Grab the cigarette holder," she instructed, and Becca picked it up. "No. Not like that," Leslie Ann said with a frown. "Hold it, you know . . ." She took the holder away from Becca, thrust out one hip and cocked her elbow, the cigarette almost to her lips, in a posture full of attitude. "Like that. Now you."

Becca struck the pose Leslie Ann had demonstrated.

"Yes!" Leslie Ann shouted. "That's perfect. See? You can do it if you try," she said as though Becca were a child learning to tie her shoes. Leslie Ann's self absorption was already getting on Becca's nerves and the evening hadn't even begun. After Leslie Ann had okayed Becca's hair and makeup, she pulled out a bottle of red wine she'd brought along to toast Becca before they got to the party. Becca found a bottle opener and four wine glasses. Chad poured.

"To Becca," Leslie Ann said raising her glass. "A great set designer. May all of your productions be under budget." As she laughed at herself, it was clear Leslie Ann had already gotten a good start on her drinking. If this party proved like every other party, Leslie Ann wouldn't be satisfied until she was completely loaded. Chad and Stephen didn't seem enthusiastic as they echoed Leslie Anne's giddy toast—"Hear, hear." Becca sipped the wine. It tasted slightly vinegary. She realized as she watched Leslie Ann that their relationship was what passed for friendship between people who didn't really know one another but thought they did. Her realization was interrupted by Leslie Ann's invitation to the guys to a tour of the house.

They tromped through the house with wine glasses in hand, exclaiming, raising eyebrows over various things until they got to the orchid room. Leslie Ann, showing off for the boys, kicked off her shoes and walked into the room. Chad and Stephen watched from the doorway with Becca. Leslie Ann was in her element: a stage and an audience. She began to improvise. "You water this thing yet?" Leslie Ann said, careening slightly toward the orchid. Becca felt her palms grow clammy. She tensed every muscle but knew enough about Leslie Ann not to give her any material, certainly not to ask her to be careful. Even without being egged on Leslie Ann now lurched forward, a mock stage trip. She appeared to catch herself and her glass of wine only inches before she crashed into the orchid and spilled the wine on the white carpet. Becca's heart pounded. She knew Leslie Ann was a skillful actress, but she found nothing funny about the scenario. Stephen laughed out loud. Becca wanted to say, "don't encourage her," but she kept her mouth shut. Finally it was Chad who intervened. "Okay, time to get on the road," he said, and turned his back on the orchid room. He's good, Becca thought. He knows exactly how to manage her. Stephen followed. Though Becca stepped away from the doorway, she waited for Leslie Ann who was visibly disappointed to have lost her audience and needed to pout a little. She quickly seemed to decide that it was a waste of time, though, and bounded out of the room with a happy grin. After she slipped on her shoes, expertly balancing her wine glass, she slid her arm through Becca's. "I'm so glad you're my friend."

Later, Becca felt bad that she didn't get a chance to tell the girls goodbye properly. Even as Leslie Ann and the guys left to wait for her in the car, the dogs seemed remote and hurt by her betrayal of them. Was that true? Hetta turned her head away as Becca moved to pet her. Although Desdemona didn't turn away she seemed confused by Hetta's reaction and suspicious of Becca.

As the car pulled away from the house, Becca could see both of the dogs watching from the living room window. "Mutt and Jeff," Stephen said. Becca wished suddenly she were staying home with the dogs.

The party was everything Becca had feared and worse. The hostess was a woman known only by her first name—Karinth. Tinkly New Age music played on the stereo and people bunched into corners watching the door critically for newcomers. Everyone seemed to know Leslie Ann. They hugged and air kissed her on both cheeks, then threw up their hands and exclaimed over her costume.

By eleven o'clock, Becca had lost three games of pool and told Chad and Stephen it was time for her to go. It would take over an hour to drive home.

"We'd better get Leslie Ann started now then," Chad said looking dubiously toward the basement ceiling as though he were seeing already the obstacle ahead of him.

Upstairs, Becca approached Leslie Ann, who was flushed with alcohol and attention. "Oh, it's the birthday girl," she said with a flamboyant hug.

"I need to be going, Leslie Ann."

"But your birthday cake. You can't leave until we've sung 'Happy Birthday.' Karinth ordered a cake especially for you."

"She shouldn't have," Becca said, feeling irritated again by Leslie Ann's insistence that this be a birthday party.

"It's your birthday. We need to sing and watch you blow out the candles."

"You're drunk, sweetie," Becca said, deciding to change tactics. "I appreciate the effort, I really do, but you promised me we'd get home by midnight."

Leslie Ann's jaw set. "We'll sing first," she said. Becca watched as each person Leslie Ann approached about the birthday celebration looked at her in confusion and said, "Who's Becca?"

Finally, by midnight there was a cake, and Becca was placed ceremoniously behind it. The candles were lit. Leslie Ann led everyone in a raucous version of "Happy Birthday" and a room full of drunk strangers clapped and cheered as Becca blew out the candles. She had never had a more miserable birthday in her life. As she bent to blow out the candles, she was tempted for a second by the dramatic vision of her fur coat catching fire in the candles. Leslie Ann had been right when she had pointed out earlier Becca was not an actress. She did not desire the stage. She thought as she blew out the candles that Leslie Ann was bad news. The worst sort of news. She knew how to act like a nice person. After all, she was an actress. Her stunning beauty made Becca, and apparently others as well, want to believe she was a nice person. But she wasn't. Becca decided she was never again going to allow Leslie Ann to talk her into anything.

When by 1:00 a.m. Leslie Ann was still not showing any signs of leaving the party, Becca tried desperately to recall the last name of Professor Blakely's friend, Alan-Who'll-Help-Out-In-A-Pinch. She had intended to bring his number for fear of the very thing that was now happening, but had left it on the kitchen counter in the flurry to leave. She was genuinely worried about the dogs and could not get out of her head Blakely's comment that they were terrified of being alone over-night. Whether that was true or not, Becca couldn't help but picture them waiting for her still by the big window in the living room, watching for her return. But an even greater fear, inspired no doubt by the reverence she felt toward it, was that something would happen to the orchid. An image flashed across her mind of Hetta lifting her leg against the plant, and Becca felt weak with anxiety. Or the white rug. How easily one of the dogs could use it instead of using the dog door to go outside.

As Becca had feared, they did not leave the party until almost 4:00 a.m. In the car going home, Leslie Ann passed out in the front seat. Becca and Stephen looked out their respective back seat windows in silence as Chad drove. It was clear to the guys and Becca that there would never be a friendship between them, and it was clear to Becca that her friendship with Leslie Ann was over.

When the car stopped to let her out, Leslie Ann roused herself. "I'll call you later."

"Don't," Becca said as she pushed open her car door.

"Don't be mad at me, honey," Leslie Ann said. "After that nice birthday celebration."

Becca exchanged a quick, understanding glance with Chad and closed the door without responding to Leslie Ann.

It was 5:00 a.m. The dogs barked as she let herself in. After putting them out, Becca turned on the lights and went immediately to the orchid room where she frantically searched the orchid for damage. When it checked out all right, she scanned the rug. She looked twice, got on her hands and knees and searched every inch. Finally, satisfied, Becca was so relieved she sank to the floor in the hallway and buried her face on her knees.

When she later let the dogs inside, it was clear Hetta was going to be slow in coming around. She turned her head away slightly from Becca. Desdemona was still confused, but Becca guessed she'd be fine once Hetta eventually forgave her. Becca understood that she could count on Hetta's forgiveness. That was the whole thing with the dogs. They wouldn't tattle on her. They were pure in that way, truly innocent. And the orchid was above emotion, the purest thing of all. Perfect.

In a day, Professor Blakely would come home. Even though nothing terrible had happened, nothing he could discern, she felt guilty. This was his family: the dogs and the orchid. She might have scoffed at that earlier, but not anymore. The dogs had taken her into their doggy world. She had had a glimpse of transcendence in the presence of the orchid. She had endangered something precious to Blakely by not honoring his wishes. There were no excuses.

Hetta nudged her hand with her little square head. "Oh, Hetta," Becca said, overcome by how quickly she had forgiven her. "Hetta." And seeing Hetta was okay again, Desdemona too came to Becca's side. The morning paper had just arrived. They all heard it at the same time as it landed with a soft thud on the front porch. Becca looked at the dogs. They followed her as she gathered the paper, and she performed the ritual for their game. Becca knew it was probably the last game of chase she would play with the dogs, and she ran with a giddy abandon through the house. She felt as though she had been given a second chance, and the feeling was not just about the white carpet and the orchid being safe, or the dogs' forgiveness. Becca couldn't say exactly what it was, only that she felt as though she had escaped something oppressive and dangerous and felt herself safe at home at last. When they had finished with the game, the girls and Becca fell together to the living room rug.

"Want a treat, girls?" Becca said after they'd rested for awhile. At the word treat, Desdemona was up and gone. She was there waiting when Becca and Hetta arrived in the kitchen. Her enormous paws were crossed slightly on the table, looking for all the world to Becca like they were folded in prayer.

The Picture in Her Dream

It was terrifying, the dream, and Gina woke in a sweat, sitting up straight in bed, feeling her heart clutch, her breathing rapid and ragged. Marcus, her husband of four years, had turned toward her, sleepy, clumsily patting her leg, you okay? falling asleep immediately not hearing her whispered yes. The next day and the next and the next the dream followed her, seemed to camp about her, oppressed her psyche like a foul odor, an obnoxious, persistent noise, and she felt as though she might never be free of it again, though what troubled her most was the fact she could remember nothing of the dream, no detail save one, and upon this single memory she had transferred all of her anxiety—a portrait, garish, its brush strokes crude, the profile of a woman, black hair pulled tight into a low braid, sallow face, red lips, a chartreuse background, the woman's solitary eye looking directly at the observer. It was not the portrait, though itself unsettling, that bothered her, but rather how it hung askance. Whatever horrifying

169

dream image she had suppressed seemed to have occurred somewhere around the disruption of the portrait, had apparently caused it to be left in its careening position.

Three days and Gina was still not able to shake the terror that the dream had inflicted. Over breakfast, the clink of silver, the clunk of glasses against the table, the sifting of newspaper pages as Marcus read while he ate his customary bowl of cereal, she brought it up again. "I can't forget the dream," she said, calling, she felt from a far off place, asking for rescue. "I'm feeling possessed by it," she said, "yes, possessed." It wasn't a mild feeling at all but rather a lost, a helpless, a frantic feeling like that of a child lost in a strange neighborhood past dark with nowhere to turn, no one to call to.

Marcus, impatient, "Just forget it, will you," turning back to his paper and his cereal, dismissing her with a final, "It's boring." She hadn't known her function was one of amusement, she snapped, and left, hurt by his disinterest. He did not apologize, did not call her back, did not take her in his arms, console, cluck over her troubles, did not say he understood, he'd had a terrible dream once, a nightmare as a child in the dark with the shadows, alone. He did not share his night terrors.

But it was not as easy to forget as Marcus had suggested. Saying forget it did not help, and the harder Gina tried to drive the fear from her, the more it persisted, dug in, left its tracks, stained everything, so that now in the evening, as she sat at the Cafe Galileo sipping her coffee, she could not concentrate to read the newspaper spread before her. The cafe was crowded, noisier than usual. A basketball game at the nearby civic center brought fans from the winning team in waves, in and out, in and out, caught up yet in the game, their voices boisterous, still filled with the cold air from outside, their laughter brittle like falling icicles.

Gina bounced one leg, nervously, distractedly, unable to stop, saturated, senses taxed. She seemed to detach then and lift from her body where she watched herself from a distance, a nail-biting distance. Had she not bounced her leg, bolted from her body, she felt she might have exploded. She winced into her skin again as a young man in a baseball cap at a table next to hers stood up, his chair scraping across the floor, his hair shaved beneath the baseball cap, wearing a white T-shirt with words in small, red letters Gina could not read inscribed over the right breast pocket. He left the chair angled out and away from the table, a broken limb, awkward, painful, disorderly, ominous, an omen. Set it right. Someone set it right. Then others were there, took the table, set it right again, a miracle she thought, and the poisonous panic that had begun to seep into her beginning with the soles of her feet and heading with focused intensity toward her heart, was arrested just in time, before it had reached its target.

She turned away, knew she was being crazy, Marcus had been right, but she couldn't seem to stop herself, her breath shallow, her eyes blinking. She looked outside for relief, where a bearded man in a trench coat walked his daughter across the street, the little girl's red velveteen coat cutting in tightly at the waist and then flaring into a skirt, beneath which hung a crescent of her dress—white eyelet. They crossed the street quickly, the traffic slowing but not to a stop, the headlights pinning the man and his child to the street, bearing down upon them, oblivious. Gina held her breath, waiting for the squeal of tires, the screams of the child, the flailing of bystanders and the swoop of the ambulance in a throb of red lights. But no, the man had made it safely across, the child in tow, and Gina wondered at her vision, the peril for which she knew she was waiting. The dream had been a warning, but she could not be prepared, retained only the urgency of premonition rather than remembered detail.

The street lights shone red in the lavender sky. It was dusk and the tops of the dark buildings hunkered above the sidewalks, in the shop windows Christmas lights, garlands of evergreen, automated dolls, a sleigh filled with wrapped presents, a Santa Claus.

"May I sit here?" a woman softly asked, startling Gina so that she did not at first respond, except to look at the woman through a haze of introspection, as if through a dirty glass. As if to apologize, the woman said all the other tables were taken in the cafe, and when Gina looked she saw it was true and gestured, "Yes, sit down, of course," polite but irritated, wanting to be alone. Gina folded the newspaper and the woman whispered, "Thanks," as she slid into the booth, set her coffee cup on the table and looked across at Gina, averting her eyes when Gina's met them, a smile, nervous and quick, a hand, hesitant, shaking, to cover her mouth when she smiled again.

Gina introduced herself, and the woman, still smiling behind her hand, said her name was Corinne. Gina nodded and looked away but had to look back again when Corinne asked, "Do you come here often?" to which Gina said noncommittally, "I guess, when I want to be quiet," meant to suggest this was one of those times. Corinne's eyes skittered away again and Gina regretted her answer, made a show of openness, "And you?" she said.

"Oh no," a breathless reply. "This is my first time," she said while surveying the room under lowered brows, quick, surreptitious glances. "I like places like this though. I like to watch people when they can't see me."

Gina smiled. "Me too," she said, "I do that too sometimes," and explained how the table they were at was best for people watching. This time when Corinne smiled she did not cover her mouth but exposed a large shelf of pale gum above small bluish teeth. Her hair, thin and dark with a few strands of gray, fell straight to her shoulders, the rims of her ears showing slightly beneath. Corinne's homeliness, almost comic to Gina, was an assurance into a kind of laughter, so much better than the sinister thoughts that had yapped relentlessly at her for days now, and she felt needy for company, for the diversion of another human being, better yet, someone she didn't know, wouldn't need to tell about the dream, as she might a friend who would notice her nervous agitation.

"Do you have a job?" Gina asked, not caring really, only wanting to hear the rhythms of conversation, the appeasement of small talk.

"Part-time. Peach Street Laundry. It's a bad job. I'm going to school—court recording," Corinne said, sipped her coffee. "Do you work?" she asked.

"At the Moon Theatre. Days during the week, nights weekends. I love films. I see them all free." Gina was enjoying this, the casual chatter, the banter of banal facts, as anonymous as sitting in the dark of the theater watching the play of form upon the screen.

"I'd like that," Corinne said, quiet a moment, seeming to weigh something she was about to say, and then, "in a movie do you think the most important things are the little things, the things most people wouldn't notice, the things you really have to watch to see?"

Gina shifted. She tugged at her sweater. "I guess that depends." She hesitated. "I'm not sure I understand exactly what you're saying, though."

Corinne, the slightest bit impatient, "like in books and stories," she said, "everyone's all caught up in the plot." She was talking quickly, a fleck of spittle on her lower lip, a spray across the table, no apology. "Everyone's all caught up in what's obvious, but no one seems to remember that the heroine one time hung her apron behind the door and straightened her dress for no real reason." A quick drink of coffee. She went on, "there's something not being said. It gets explained away. Just movement. Meant to create a realistic setting, to move the action forward, but that answer isn't right. And it happens in real life too."

Gina frowned. "I don't think I quite understand."

The impatience again. "It's like this . . ." And Corinne went on to describe something about a party once where the host had worn blue bedroom slippers, a convoluted story that Gina heard only in pieces, becoming fascinated with the fact that Corinne's skin was flawless, pale, like china, a bluish undertone.

Once the story was finished Gina sipped her coffee, did not reply, looked back out onto the street where a boy in a black parka ran by holding a paper bag at arm's length, and two women dressed in suits and no coats walked in stride, one laughing at something the other had said, their breath coming in short bursts of fog.

"I suppose you know all about movies," Corinne said.

Gina pulled her eyes back to the table. She shrugged. "A little, I suppose. And you?"

"Me?" Corinne laughed in the same whispering, breathless way she talked. "Not at all really. I wasn't allowed to go when I was young. I like them, but I don't go very often."

"Why weren't you allowed to go?"

"My religion. Adventist," Corinne said, her voice

suddenly sharp as though Gina was silly not to have known. Corinne frowned. The frown faded. "I'd like to tell my mother about you," she said then and sighed. "I haven't met anyone I like for the longest time, but I'd have to lie something awful. We're in a coffee house, you know, and it's Sabbath, and you work in a theater. I just wouldn't feel comfortable lying that much. I'd feel even worse not telling her all the details, though, because like I said earlier, that's what I think is most important. So, I won't be able to tell her. It's always that way."

Gina did not respond, felt leeched and weak, wished she had not entered the conversation. The sky had grown dark. Darker still were the clouds massed and lurking, finger-like, behind the buildings to the west. Looking into that darkness Gina felt a chill shudder through her, the warning, the wariness, so that when she turned her eyes back to the table and saw how Corinne was watching her, a greedy, searching expression, Gina felt as though she couldn't breathe, as though she needed to leave the cafe. With all the force of panic she felt she must go. Brusquely, "I need to be going," she said as she drained her cup of the last of its tepid coffee.

"Already?" Corinne asked.

"I'm afraid so."

"Do you have to work?" Corinne pressed.

"No. I just need to be going."

Corinne's face brightened, spread out, moonlike and white. "I couldn't invite you to my apartment," she said, "because of what I told you about my mother, but I could go to your house, walk home with you. I wouldn't have to tell her that. She doesn't need to know I wasn't just out walking and happened to go a little further than usual, stayed out a little later than usual."

"I'm sorry, but my husband is expecting me," Gina said and stood up. "We have plans tonight."

Corinne pressed her lips together. Her narrowed eyes refused to meet Gina's. "I see," she said through tight lips. "And it wouldn't be possible for me to meet him, to stop in for a while?" She said it angrily and looked at Gina then. "No, of course not. It wouldn't be possible to introduce us. Of course not," she repeated tersely, her voice rising.

Gina saw that several people in the cafe had stopped talking to look. She wanted to quiet Corinne and saw it was going to be difficult. She couldn't think, couldn't muster the wit to wriggle out of this, somehow couldn't face the scene, the criticism, the energy for this. Perhaps a quick visit, a brief introduction to Marcus. What could it hurt? "I guess it'd be okay to introduce you," she said then.

At this, Corinne immediately relaxed. She beamed. "Really. You mean it?" Gina nodded. They left their empty cups in the bus tub on their way out. Gina felt Corinne close against her heels as she pushed out the door.

Outside, the sound of traffic, the blare and blur of sound, felt good to Gina, the cold a pleasurable pain, the moving of muscles, sinew, cartilage, all very clear, everything clear, the moving joints, the minute creaking, the hum and order of the body in motion, the blood washing through, the field of skin mere points of nerve, plaited and held together by what? She didn't know, couldn't think that far, only wanted to be away, walking away, alone, and Corinne there close at her elbow taking small running steps to keep up with her. Gina shoved her hands deep into her coat pockets, put her head down, drove against the wind, determined, until Corinne bumped against her in her frantic desire to stay close. Dread. Drowning in dread. What had she gotten herself into? How had it happened, the stifling need to be close, to belong, to fit?

She stopped then, suddenly, surprising herself, and faced Corinne. In confusion, Corinne shuffled on for a few feet in that running way.

"I'm afraid I can't let you come home with me," Gina said before Corinne had quite stopped. The wind whipped the words out of her mouth, flung them back at her.

"But you said . . ." Corinne began, scolding, frowning, formidable.

"I know, but it's the picture, in my dream, a dream I had three nights ago, it's bothered me since. You said it yourself, it's the little thing that becomes the whole, and this isn't right." Gina said it in a rush nearly incoherent, her mouth numb with cold, her tongue thick, a fish flopping in desperation.

"Yes, I see," Corinne interrupted. "You should have said something about the dream sooner." Then, abruptly, without a word of farewell, Corinne left. No resistance. No ugly scene. Corinne was gone. Gina watched as the darkness met and enveloped her, seemed to welcome her, take her in, a friend long gone pulled into waiting arms. Gina felt unbalanced. Expecting a fight, she had geared up for it, planted and braced herself. Now there was nothing. Nothing at all. With Corinne had also gone the menacing thoughts, the dream anxiety. No more presentiment. No more terror. No more waiting for disaster. Only the sensation of feathers recently ruffled, the silence after a window is shattered, the scream of a train in the night receding now, a passing shock.

Billy

The shades were still drawn when Mary arrived home. In the dim living room the television flickered soundlessly. Strewn across the floor were soiled dishes, sections of the newspaper, and piles of empty bottles. There on the brown couch, springs sagging to the floor, wool upholstery nappy and soiled, asleep amid the chaos, was Mary's husband, William. The brown couch had been their first purchase as newlyweds. Even brand new sitting in the furniture store's showroom Mary had not liked it. She had wanted instead the pale yellow couch with the flowered tapestry pillows displayed in the store window. But there had been no discussion about the couch. "I'm not going to have a bunch of prissy shit cluttering up my house," William had said.

Mary was the only one who called him William. To everyone else he was Billy. Mary's refusal to call him Billy had confused him at first, and she supposed now that her reasons for calling him William were pretentious at worst and hopeful at best. She had wanted a husband who stood apart, someone different from the locals who hung around at Decker's Saloon in downtown Sweetwater. She had wanted someone with ambition to match her own, someone who would be a ticket to the dreams she had for travel and knowledge and that worldly sophistication she found so attractive in others and so elusive in her own life.

With one more glance around the living room Mary turned off the television and went to the kitchen. She had barely seen William on the couch, and he had not stirred at her presence. Her eyes had swept around the room and noted him along with all the other turmoil. By now, William and the worn, brown couch had become one. Disappointment in him no longer registered as an emotion. Everyone who knew Mary—the townspeople, her family—might have described her as resigned but not as a martyr, for she neither reveled in William's failure nor railed against it. Rather, for years she had avoided him, often dreaming of the time when she would leave him.

From the refrigerator, Mary took a package of bologna, a block of cheese, and a jar of mustard and proceeded to make a sandwich. She did not bother to make anything for William, who she guessed would stay passed out for the remainder of the night. In the evenings, there was usually evidence that William had been in the kitchen scavenging for food during the day while she was gone. Tonight the place looked surprisingly neat.

Mary switched on the radio and sat down at the gray Formica table. From the oldies station, Andy Williams's voice filled the cold, empty kitchen like warm water, like a warm bath, Mary thought. She decided to soak in the tub after her meal. As a child, in her mother's house, she had bathed each Saturday night in the big claw-foot tub. Afterward, wrapped in a thick, flannel robe, she had stood between her mother's legs to have her hair combed straight then sectioned and wound into pin curls. She could still smell Prell shampoo and Dippity Do and the slightly pungent, sweet musk rising from her mother's spread legs.

Mary checked the living room again before going upstairs. She glimpsed William through the darkness. A brief sense of something like tenderness skipped across her heart, such a fleeting sensation she could barely recall having felt it. It was his vulnerable position, the way he lay there so exposed, so helpless. Yet she knew if William found out she was really leaving him this time he would find a way to stop her. She marveled now at his trust. If he knew the real harm she had wished him through the years he would never have slept like that. But who was she kidding? William had always been safe. Mary had represented no threat to William. She was the one who was helpless, exposed, vulnerable. He had tracked her relentlessly and struck with consistent precision at her weakest spots. She remembered now how she had first loved William with a trembling, quivering trust. In the past she thought William had been right when he told her she was lucky to have married at all. She thought he had been right too when he told her she had been spoiled, a spoiled girl, but she knew now William had been wrong all along.

Her parents' comments before the wedding had suggested their concerns about the marriage. "He's the best goddamned mechanic I know, but he has the manners of a monkey," her father had gone so far to say one time. Mary had adored William and had wanted to protect him from her parents' criticism. By the time she realized the truth of their fears she had had her first child and no way to raise her by herself. At least that was what she told herself at the time. She told herself she didn't want to disgrace her parents by leaving the marriage. Through the years she had told herself a lot of things. No more though.

Later, in the bathtub, she sank to her chin in the steaming water. Only the nightlight lit the room. Even in its soft glow she could see the signs of her aging— small liver spots on her hands, her skin slightly papery, the muscles lax about the elbows. She did not mourn her loss of youth but rather the loss of time. What had she hoped for? She couldn't remember now. She had dreamt the dreams of all young girls, she imagined— romance, passion, possessions. They had been silly dreams. But how was she to have known that then? Everything around her had encouraged only one role— wife and mother. More simply put, a woman's success was measured by how well she married. Why should she have been better than her time? Why should she have seen through? Suddenly there in the bathtub Mary felt angry down to her toes. The force of her rage took her by surprise, she so rarely allowed herself such luxury of emotion. She hadn't felt it there inside, waiting, and almost wished she could be there to see William's face when he read her note the day after tomorrow.

Beneath her, the water gently rocked against the sides of the tub. She sighed and lowered her arms back into the water.

She had met William the summer she graduated from high school. He had swaggered into her father's shop and asked for a job as a mechanic. Mary had watched as her father squinted in that way he did when he was sizing up someone. After a few minutes he had wiped his palms on his greasy overalls and said he could use a hand here and there.

Mary hadn't known what to make of William. His fingernails were black with grease, and his clothes were outdated and worn. But he was handsome. He wore his dark, wavy hair slicked back. He had strong, white teeth and a voluptuous mouth. When he smiled his lip curled. How could she resist?

William was ten years older than she and had traveled across the U.S. before coming back home to Sweetwater. Mary had given in to him, given up the whole of her heart, not by degrees but in one moment of submersion, a complete and shuddering surrender.

The bath water had grown tepid. Mary added more

hot water. She tensed then, and lay very still. For a second she imagined she had heard William stir downstairs, but no. Everything was quiet and dark. Mary questioned her slightly racing heart, the desire she still felt for William at times, the way, in unguarded moments, she seemed yet to hope for a response from him. Strange how his disinterest still hurt sometimes.

Mary thought about Don then. Steady, good-hearted, reliable Don. She didn't feel that head over heels, butterflies in the belly love she had felt with William, but Don made her feel safe, and Mary wanted that now more than anything.

At first Mary had wanted to be a perfect wife. She had tried to keep a spotless house like her mother's, but she had not been trained for the job and could never seem to get organized. It was difficult to dress well on their small income, though she was puzzled by where the money went; she was certain her father paid William well. Then the children came and the effort grew strained beyond her limits. She felt the corners of her life erode as William's habits became more erratic—staying out all night, drinking with buddies all weekend. She had cried and thrown tantrums but to no effect. William made no concession to her demands.

When her father died and William took over the business things went well for a few months, but the old habits resurfaced and the business began to fail. That was when Mary took a job at Beacon Enterprises as a temporary solution. Thirty years later she was still there. She had turned down offers to advance in the company. Things were bound to change next year, she had told herself. Year to year she had lived in the moment, expecting the inevitable turn around. William would awaken again to her and his responsibilities, and life would be good in a way it had never been good.

Now and then in the early years, William would come to her maudlin and apologetic. "You're too good," he would say. "You and the kids would be better off without me." Then he would beg her not to go. In the meantime, through her long wait, the children grew up and left. They called but seldom came home and seemed to find refuge in their own lives. Sometimes the children felt like ghosts to Mary, distant memories.

The ringing phone startled her. She crawled out of the now chilly bath water and toweled off as she ran to answer it.

"Billy there?"

"Yes, but he's asleep, Elvin."

"Well then, goddammit, wake him up." Elvin laughed with a wheeze.

Mary did not reply.

"When he comes to, have him call." The phone clicked and the line went dead. Mary shivered and finished drying off.

Once in her warm robe, she went back downstairs to make a cup of cocoa. She did not like being downstairs in the evening. It was not the dust and cobwebs, the stacks of newspapers and clothes that bothered her, but rather the eerie feeling of being so near someone who couldn't acknowledge she existed.

When the oldest child, her daughter Rojene, had left seven years earlier, Mary had taken her bedroom for herself. Beside the bed she kept a small television, a radio, and a recliner. Across the back of the recliner hung a green afghan her daughter Chris had made for her several Christmases before. The chair springs groaned when Mary sat down, and the cushion sank unevenly to one side. The afghan felt good across her shoulders as she watched reruns of television sitcoms.

The phone again. She must have fallen asleep. Her heart thudded in her chest. She was slow to answer it.

"Can you talk?" It was Don.

Mary glanced quickly into the dark hall, a nervous reflex since she knew William would not be up. "Why are you calling? William could have picked up."

"I know. I just needed to make some last minute arrangements."

Mary smiled. Don's organization and care of detail. "All right, but hurry though." She couldn't think why she was feeling so fidgety.

"We're booked for a 10:00 a.m. flight on Friday, but when I called to reconfirm, the airline said they have some openings on an 8:00 a.m. flight if we want to switch."

"No," Mary said, feeling suddenly panicked about any changes to the plan.

"Okay, that's fine," Don said.

"It's just that William might be suspicious. He might catch on if I left too early. I want him to think I'm going to work is all. We can't do anything to jinx ourselves here."

Don laughed. "Quit worrying. Everything'll be okay, Mary. We'll be in Cleveland by Friday afternoon. We'll find new jobs and start over. You watch. It'll be okay."

"I know," she said, though she felt it was all too fragile, maybe too good to be true. She hadn't liked the months of sneaking around, deceiving Don's wife, Charlene, avoiding William.

The temperature dropped below zero the following evening. Mary drove home from work in a howling wind. It beat against the car. The house was dark as she pulled into the drive. The stillness seemed ominous and Mary shuddered slightly. She was tempted not to go inside but had nowhere else to go, belonged nowhere but to that house. Don would be at his house with his wife and children. He could be of no help to her. If she could just get through one more night. Tomorrow they would be in Cleveland.

Mary stumbled on the stairs inside the side door. The house seemed unusually dark. Once she had glanced into the living room she realized it was the television. The lack of its blue light accounted for the darkness. To set things right she turned it on. In its flickering glow she observed the same dishes, the same newspapers, the same bottles that had been there the night before. She looked at William then, his body sprawled on the couch, one arm hanging over the edge, his hand just brushing the floor. It was the same posture she had seen him in night after night for years, but somehow she saw it was different tonight, the sprawl slightly wooden, the skin waxy white. As Mary inched a little nearer she felt the hairs rise on her arms.

Later, she guessed she knew before she saw the gaping, breathless mouth and the hollow eyes, half open, staring blankly at the ceiling, that William was dead.

"It's finally over then, is it?" Mary heard herself say. Her voice sounded hoarse and loud, unfamiliar to her.

Shadows from the television played across William's face. Mary held her hand over his eyes for a moment. She was surprised at her calm. She sank to the floor beside the couch. While avoiding the staring eyes, she looked at William, noting his unshaven cheeks and chin, his wide nose with its triangular shaped nostrils, his thick salt-and-pepper eyebrows, and his still sensual lips. Mary reached out a tentative hand then and touched him lightly. Just her fingertips grazed his shirt. At last she laid her hand against his chest. The body felt cold, unresponsive. A sickly sweet smell clung to the skin. Mary guessed William had been dead for a long time. She stroked his chest slightly. Only as she realized how long it had been since she had touched him did she weep. She was taken aback by her grief, but she gave in to it and laid her head upon William's chest and cried like she might have cried against her father's shoulder when she was a child, heaving sobs. She was not frightened of the corpse as she would have expected. All she wanted was to preserve the stillness a while longer.

When she had first fallen in love with William, first felt that opening, that soft melting toward him, Mary believed it was a miracle, a rebirth. He had walked with her one humid evening after the cicadas had hushed their keening, after the fireflies had found their mates and extinguished their beckoning lights, in the fretful hours past dark in the lingering heat of a Nebraska summer. They found themselves by the river at the edge of Sweetwater, under a wooden bridge covered with graffiti—"Bobcats '57," "Harry + Bonnie=Love." The water nudged against the crumbling bank with a slight sucking sound. And there, amidst the lapping water and the bullfrog's dirge, she felt William's arms circle her from behind. She had never felt so solid, so certain she was of this world and meant to be, as in that moment.

Outside the wind moaned. The house felt cold as the windows shook. The thought of police cars and ambulances and EMTs coming in the night, disrupting the quiet, was more than Mary could bear. Moving William's body in the cold of this dark night felt wrong too, disrespectful. Mary was puzzled by the gentleness she felt as she softly pushed William's hair away from his face.

All the anger. Where was the anger? For the moment it had been replaced with a calm, almost ritualized resolve. The thought came to Mary that William had not ruined her life; she had allowed her life to be ruined. It was a pity, a waste. What possible good would it do to look back now? She had been looking back too long, she realized, wishing, resisting. Their life together would not bear scrutiny.

She did not call Don. Somehow she felt cut off from the new life she had meant to start because of the old life she needed to mourn. She did not think it strange that she sat through the night with William's body, dozing, waking to weep now and then. She wanted to defy the modern world's antiseptic preoccupation to dispose of the dead with haste, and kept watch with William's body through the night just as she imagined women throughout history had kept vigil with the dead, had mourned with the whole of humanity through the long, dark nights of death.

At the first light of day a spell seemed to break. Mary washed her face and phoned the emergency number. She dialed Don's number, thankful it was he who answered.

"Hey," he said when he heard her voice. "D-day."

"That's why I'm calling."

"What?" She heard the caution in Don's voice, the way he seemed to back away slightly as though protecting himself.

"It's William."

"What'd the bastard do now?" Don said in a whisper.

"He's dead," Mary said. "We'll have to wait," she went on.

"Shit," Don said.

"I've got to go. The ambulance will be here soon." In the distance Mary could hear the sirens.

William's body was covered and loaded into the ambulance with a show of lights. Police officers and the coroner's staff searched the house and asked Mary questions. They scribbled reports and filed away—blue suit after blue suit. Mary stood in the doorway, in the cold, sharp light of a January morning and watched the uniformed people. Then she was alone.

That afternoon a deputy from the county attorney's office returned to the house. A young man wearing a shiny new wedding ring. He was younger than Mary's older children, eager and hesitant. Mary guessed it was his first job out of law school. The young man stammered and looked uncomfortable as he told Mary that the time of death had been established in the morning hours two days previous. "For purposes of our investigation we'll need to know your whereabouts during the past two days."

"I was at work each day, home by six. I've been at home in the evenings."

"You were at home?" The young man frowned.

"That's right," Mary said.

"And you didn't notice anything?" His voice

rebuked her. Mary wanted to smile. In a short time, with practice, she knew, the young man would culti-vate a curt, disinterested demeanor with which to pose such questions.

"That's right," Mary said again. No explanations. How could she explain?

"I'm afraid I find that implausible, Ma'am."

Mary shrugged. "It's how it was."

The matter was dropped: cause of death clearly ad-vanced and neglected cirrhosis of the liver.

The following day the children arrived early. They made the funeral arrangements and settled the insur-ance claims. They ordered a gravestone upon which they inscribed their father's name, "Billy Rush." Mary did not argue with their choice. They stayed for five days. Before they left, the children sorted and gave away their father's things, paid the bills, and cleaned the house.

After the last one had gone Mary walked through the silent and orderly rooms as though she were in a stranger's house. She felt ill at ease for awhile, then she smiled and patted the kitchen wall. "Mine," she said aloud. It made her laugh. "My house." She breathed deeply. She walked through each room touching cup-boards and countertops, door knobs and end tables all with the corresponding mantra "Mine, mine!" Only as she came to the brown couch did her smile drop. The couch defied her possession with its sagging springs, the sour smell emanating from its stained brown upholstery. It would have to go first thing. She smiled at her decisiveness.

Don had asked to come over once the children left. From the living room window Mary watched now as his Ford Taurus pulled up to the curb. Don got out. He leaned back into the car to take something from the backseat and then he stood up again and adjusted his coat. Now that Don was actually here, she realized she hadn't missed him. She opened the door for him as he stepped onto the porch. He smiled as he stomped his boots on the porch trying to warm himself. They kissed clumsily once he was inside the door.

"Here. This is for you," he said pushing a brown paper bag toward her. He immediately dropped to one knee after she took the bag from him and began to remove his boots.

"Don't worry about those," she said. "Come on in. I'll make coffee." Only after she'd spoken did she take note of the bag she was holding. She opened the top. Inside were two loaves of home baked bread. "Did you . . . Are these from . . . ?"

Don nodded. "Charlene baked those for you. She figured you'd have a houseful," he added blushing. "She sends her sympathy."

"Oh. That's nice of her. The kids were all here, but they're gone now," Mary said. "I'll freeze one."

Don looked startled. "You'll freeze one?"

Mary set her mouth and nodded. "Yes, for later. I'll use it later."

"I see," Don said, his eyes shifting away from hers.

"Maybe we can talk in a week or so," Mary said, wanting to soften the tone of things.

Don's face reddened. She didn't know if it was in anger or embarrassment. "I understand," he repeated. Then, "I better be going."

"Okay." Mary felt relieved as the door closed behind him. She couldn't explain her changed feelings. Somehow what she felt for Don had died with Billy. Perhaps later they could rekindle their romance, but for now she felt content to be alone.

Mary noticed then it had started to snow. She watched as a drift formed on the outside sill of the front room window. A fragile lip of soft snow extended beyond the sill and threatened to break away. She thought about how clean and cold the falling snow would feel on her upturned face, how she would be startled by the cold at first, and then how she would grow accustomed to it, how she would revel in its newness.

This Is Not the Tropics

"There are many kinds of love in the world! Happy Valentine's Day! Love, Daddy." Charlotte put the tiny card back into its envelope just as the typewriter repairman knocked on the door.

"Good morning." Charlotte held the door open for his tool cart.

"There'll be a foot of snow by nightfall," the man said. Large wet flakes of snow stuck to his head and to the broad shoulders of his gray wool coat. Once inside, he wiped snow off his cart.

Charlotte shivered as she looked outside. "Thanks for coming so quickly."

"No problem. There was no guarantee I'd get here if I waited until later today."

"The typewriter's over here." The repairman followed Charlotte, the wheels of his tool cart bumping loudly over the linoleum floor.

"Well, aren't you special," the man said as he saw

the roses beside her desk. "I've never seen so many roses before. Is that a dozen?"

"Two dozen."

The man whistled softly. "Somebody must really love you."

"It's not what it seems." Charlotte said. "They're not—I don't have a boyfriend."

The repairman nodded. He took off his coat and hung it over the back of the chair. Underneath he wore a suit and tie. "So, you have plans for tonight?" he asked and smiled at Charlotte.

"Oh, no," she said.

After the repairman started work on her typewriter, Charlotte left him to put the assembly room in order before Helen and Kevin arrived to start work. The shop was quiet now in the hours before they opened for business. She did a quick inventory: She'd need to order a box of small pedestals and more screws for the larger plaques. She swept the floor again even though Kevin and Helen supposedly swept it each night before closing. Things were never left quite as she would like. Charlotte was the manager of the store, had been for eleven years. Before that, she worked for six years in the assembly room.

When she first took the job at Capital Trophy, Russell had been working there. He left a couple years later to live in an Exodus House in San Raphael with nine other young men who were also trying to stop being gay. Before he left, Russell told her he was doing it for religious reasons. She hadn't been aware that he was religious. Actually, until right before he left she hadn't been aware he was gay. Charlotte still couldn't quite grasp his motive for the Exodus House fiasco, unless it was part of his obsession at the time with sexual histories. When Lyle, the guy who replaced him, found out why Russell had left, he whooped, "He's what?" And he made Charlotte say it again. "That's too goddamned precious," he said. "That's like me deciding I'm going to quit being a heterosexual by going to live in a house with a bunch of twenty-year-old women."

Charlotte didn't have a real opinion about what Russell was doing at that time. He had always been changeable by her way of thinking, and her role in their friendship was mainly to listen. Russell was her friend, though, and she had felt she needed to defend him against Lyle's criticism. The problem was, she didn't know how. She'd wished a million times afterward she'd never told Lyle where Russell had been going. Now and then, if he ran into her, Lyle still ribbed Charlotte about Russell. "That friend of yours still trying not to be gay?"

That was a long time ago. Russell had long since left the Exodus House. Unsurprisingly, he had been kicked out within a couple of months. He was in Finland now. He'd met a man and gone to stay with him for six months. In the postcards he sent, he sounded happy. Charlotte had figured, being so far away, he'd forget her this Valentine's Day. She had been surprised when the flowers came first thing after she arrived at the shop that morning.

The repairman closed the top of her IBM Selectric with a firm snap. "That should do you," he said. He carefully put away the few tools he had taken out and closed and clasped his tool kit. The little glimpse she had inside the tool kit pleased Charlotte—everything in its place, orderly. She liked order. She figured it was what made her a good manager. The repairman put on his coat and glanced outside. "She's really coming down."

Charlotte shivered again and hugged her arms. "Makes me want to go someplace warm."

"Isn't that the truth." The repairman reached for his coat. He jutted his chin toward Charlotte. "That why you're dressed like that today?"

Charlotte glanced down, as though she'd forgotten what she was wearing—a sleeveless tangerine blouse and lime green pants. She'd given it no thought that morning; it was what looked comfortable.

"See you," the repairman said as he headed toward the front door.

"I hope not for a while. No offense."

"I understand. I wouldn't want to see me coming either."

Almost as soon as Charlotte turned the sign from Closed to Open, the first customer, a woman, walked in. The woman wore a long black leather coat and a taupe-colored silk scarf. Her hair was dyed a rich mink color and thick gold hoops hung from her ears. She stood just inside the door of the shop and looked around as she slowly pulled off her gloves, giving little tugs at each fingertip first. Charlotte looked around, too, seeing the shop as the woman might. A large window covered much of the wall adjacent to the door. Stenciled letters arced in the window—Capital Award and Trophy. There were no other windows in the showroom. Display shelves held various sorts and sizes of trophies, award cups, paperweights and pyramids, all bearing inscription plaques. On the back wall were wall plaques, framed commemorative certificates, hanging wooden and metal awards with carved or etched detailing.

The shop's linoleum floor was worn in places. The walls, though recently painted white, were nonetheless in bad shape. Charlotte had spoken to the owner about her concerns that the showroom needed to be renovated. She wasn't disturbed by its appearance every day, but customers, such as the woman whose gaze had now reached as far as the counter behind which Charlotte stood, would occasionally remind her how shabby it looked.

When the woman's eyes met Charlotte's, Charlotte smiled and walked around the counter. "Was there something in particular you were looking for?"

The woman didn't say anything for a second as she

glanced around the showroom once more and then quickly took in Charlotte as well. "I'm looking for something, nothing big really, to commemorate Lawrence Bigby's ten years as president of Friends of the Symphony. You're probably aware we're having a dinner to honor him in a few weeks."

Charlotte had no knowledge of the event to which the woman referred. She said, "Were you looking for a standing or a hanging commemorative?"

"Hanging, I should think."

Charlotte walked toward the back wall. She felt the woman walking closely behind her. Once they'd stopped, the woman pulled out of her purse a pair of half glasses and looked intently at the assortment of wall-mounted models. Letting the glasses slide down her nose, the woman finally looked over the top of them at Charlotte.

"Do you have something, something more— understated. More on the elegant side?"

"Elegant," Charlotte repeated. She glanced around the room as if searching, though she knew these were the only models they had. "I'm sorry," she said finally, shaking her head. "We could make something to spec if you'd like."

The woman briskly took off her glasses, folded and replaced them in her purse. "I'll take that information back to the committee." The woman's extended hand surprised Charlotte, who found her hand grasped and shaken once brusquely. "Thank you for your time."

Before the woman had quite released Charlotte's hand, the door to the assembly room burst open and Kevin walked into the showroom still shouting something over his shoulder. "They can just go fuck themselves," he said before noticing Charlotte and the woman. "Whoops," he said and set down the trophy he was holding, a bowler atop a round base with a gold plaque that read "The Rips, 1998 Champions," on the shelf designated To Be Delivered. He mouthed, "Sorry," to Charlotte when the woman looked away. His sleeves were rolled back to reveal hairy forearms, a tattoo on each, one of a coiled snake, the other of a rising sun. He ducked back into the assembly room. After a few seconds interval there was a yelp of laughter from Helen, no doubt a response to having just heard about Kevin's blunder.

Once the woman left, Charlotte sat down to work on invoices. The roses gave off a heavy funereal perfume. She moved the vase off her desk to a credenza nearby. Sometimes she wished she'd never told Russell anything. Roses were definitely not Russell's style, nor were they hers. There was something stubborn and morbid about the roses, coming each year. There was something vindictive about them too. Russell knew Charlotte wouldn't really like roses, especially not so many, but since they never spoke about his annual gesture, she could never tell him her feelings. Actually, she didn't need to talk to him about it at all. Russell knew well their effect. He could never just give a simple gift;

everything he did he thought about intensely—every detail perfect. Russell was the sort of guy capable of sending beautiful spring flowers. Why not two dozen daffodils? She knew he sent roses because he liked the campiness of the traditional red roses for passion. He knew all too well the effect two dozen would create, enough roses to cover a casket. So what was his point? Passion was equivalent with death? Too much passion was sickening/overwhelming? This from a man who built his life around passions of one sort or another? Charlotte knew with anyone else she might be reading too much into the gift, but with Russell there could never be enough second guessing.

When she and Russell first met, Charlotte thought he was handsome and funny, and he was the first man she'd ever known who didn't make her nervous. Now, looking back, it should have been obvious to her that he was gay, but it wasn't. Russell wasn't immediately forthcoming about it either. Charlotte had thought then it was because he had been shy, afraid she might not like him as well if she knew. Now she knew him well enough to know it hadn't been that at all. He didn't tell her immediately because he liked her adoration. He liked it that she had a crush on him. He still did. The last time she saw him, right before he left for Finland, he had looked magnificent: a cinnamon-colored linen shirt, an embroidered Laotian vest, chinos. His hair, graying at the temples, was cut close, and he wore a goatee, also graying. He was growing old in a good way, she had thought. He had known she would appreciate him. Sometimes, she suspected it was her dowdiness and lack of sophistication that he most liked about her, for the way it offset his urbane and worldly style. Russell had thrown a fit when he saw her, as she knew he would.

"What are you thinking, Charlotte?" he had said as he lifted her thin hair from where it fell past her shoulders. "This needs to go. It's not the '70s, dearie."

Charlotte had laughed nervously as she always did when Russell made suggestions for improvement. He clucked over her outdated clothes. "You know," he had said, "you could be a knockout if you just put a little effort into the business."

"That's just it, Russell," she had said. "I'm not into that. It takes too much effort." Charlotte could always tell he was itching to orchestrate her make over. Strangely enough, Russell's eternal criticisms of her never made her feel pathetic. They instead made her feel valued, as though she were someone of potential beauty who chose to be unattractive. Maybe it was for that precise reason she never took the steps to improve herself that Russell suggested, all of them reasonable enough, because if she followed through and she were still plain, then what? By its nature it would have to be a disappointment, and that, she could never bear, Russell's silent and polite acquiescence to her inevitable plainness.

By this time, Charlotte knew Russell so well she felt sometimes he possessed her. She caught herself more often than she liked hearing his sarcastic or approving response to some incident. It was maddening how a strong personality such as his could so completely bowl over a personality like hers. Charlotte felt sure Russell never saw the world, even momentarily, through her eyes, but just when she had convinced herself she would disappear from his memory, like when he left for Finland, Russell would do something to remind Charlotte she was still his friend. She had been sure the flowers wouldn't arrive this year. How could anyone send flowers from Finland? Why would he? And yet here they were as they had been every Valentine's Day for seventeen years.

While making entries in the ledger book, the lead in her mechanical pencil broke. Charlotte's efforts to move the lead forward were frustrated. Even changing the lead did no good, and in the end she threw the pencil with disgust into the metal garbage can near her desk. It rang against the sides of the can. She hadn't noticed Helen and Kevin standing behind her until she heard Helen's barking laugh.

"You startled me," Charlotte said.

"You seem a little flustered today, Charlotte," Helen said. Charlotte didn't answer her.

"Sorry about that earlier," Kevin said. The two of them laughed again.

"You two sure are in a mood today."

"Now that you bring it up," Helen said and giggled. "We are in a mood."

Charlotte had lost interest. She straightened the finished invoices on her desk.

"Aren't you even curious, Charlotte?" Kevin asked.

Charlotte looked up again. "About what?"

"Us?"

Charlotte shook her head. "What about you?"

Laughter again. Kevin bent at the waist as though in pain from the mirth of it. Helen let out one of her signature yelps as she held out her left hand. On the ring finger was a large pink plastic ring with a heart inscribed "Be My Love." The word "Love" had been crossed out and in magic marker had been substituted in tiny letters "Wife." Charlotte glanced quickly from the ring to Helen's and Kevin's smiling, waiting faces. They laughed again at Charlotte's expression.

"You should see yourself," Kevin said, apparently delighted with the effect.

"I . . ." Charlotte started.

"We're engaged," Helen said.

"Yes. I gathered as much," Charlotte said. "Well . . . congratulations."

"Thanks," Kevin said and straightened up slightly, his expression growing more serious. "We'll want some time off, a week in . . ." he hesitated and glanced with a questioning look at Helen. "June?"

"June." Helen nodded.

"That's fine. Of course," Charlotte said, though neither Kevin nor Helen seemed to have heard her response. They left without saying anything more to her, swinging their clasped hands together like children.

The shop seemed even dingier as she watched Kevin and Helen. How was it she hadn't noticed the dust everywhere? How was it she hadn't noticed Kevin and Helen getting this serious about each other? How had such things escaped her? She really couldn't . . . she couldn't. She always had the feeling that for every effort forward, entropy was taking things two steps back. She hated that awareness, hated the sense that time was passing along in its destructive way and here she was foraging through her desk drawer in search of another mechanical pencil, the search for a pencil as fraught with importance at this second as any other search. Such silly thoughts. Where did they come from? These she couldn't blame on Russell. They'd always been with her, marauding little thoughts that seemed to leave her feeling belittled and pathetic.

When she and Russell had worked together as assemblers they had laughed and talked, always cutting up. All day they had time to talk. They must have made the then manager, Mr. Delvaney, Old Delvaney, as they always called him, crazy. Russell had been obsessively curious about anything sexual in those days. When they first met, he had pried her for sexual secrets. She'd never encountered anyone like him before or since. He was exploring the dark world of sex then like other people traveled. He bought books, found addresses, met others with information, and brought the stories of his adventures back to her. Charlotte knew more about lap dancers and S&M and butt plugs and sexual fetishes than she could ever want to know. Her mind was a repository for this information, odd details of which sometimes still appeared in her dreams. She couldn't deny Russell's stories had been riveting, but she was terribly uncomfortable with them, too, and Russell knew it. Part of the fun of discovery for him was her squeamishness at hearing his tales. He was, as far as she thought then, not a participant in these activities, but an avid observer only.

Part of his inquiry included what he liked to call sexual histories. He was never shy about asking Charlotte questions about her sexual past, and she had been too young then to know she didn't need to answer every question posed to her. He shortly discovered she was still a virgin. She could feel him practically salivate over that information. She didn't know yet, as she would know later, that the thought of actually having sex with a woman made him sick. She thought he was fascinated because he was interested in her. Even now, after all these years, he was still fascinated by her virginity, which if at twenty-three was interesting, at forty was downright amazing in Russell's eyes. He contradicted himself all the time when it came to her virginity, though. On one hand, he told her she should get rid of it immediately. Just have done with it. It was holding her back. On the other hand, she could tell, it was the one quality about her that genuinely intrigued him still.

Russell had lost his virginity when he was twelve with a PE teacher in seventh grade. When Charlotte responded in horror, had said something about child abuse and molestation, Russell laughed at her. "Wasn't anybody taking advantage of me, Missy. I seduced him. I wanted it."

"Why?"

"Why? Because that's how I'm made. I like men, and I knew that at a really young age. By twelve I was so horny I couldn't stand myself. I could tell Mr. Jacobs leaned the same direction and that's all there was to it. If anything, he was my victim." And then Russell laughed in a wicked way.

Charlotte hadn't said anything at the time. She was completely shocked both by his coming out and by his secret. When he asked what she was doing when she was twelve, she told him about the Valentine's Day dance, 1972. She and her friend Nancy, giddy all through Math, the last period of the day. They were going to their first boy/girl dance. As she was telling this story, she felt what a far cry it was from Russell's experience. Her naivete embarrassed her even then, but she went on, wanting to give Russell something, to even the score. Charlotte thought then that things worked in those ways, you tell me your secret, I'm obligated to tell mine.

That night at the dance things did not go as Charlotte had hoped. From the first moment they arrived, the boys were as attentive to Nancy as they were inattentive to Charlotte. As quickly as one dance ended Nancy was invited to dance again, leaving Charlotte to shrink farther and farther with each dance undanced against the beige walls of the gym. Not one offer all night except one near the end, a handsome boy named Brad who had dominated Nancy's time that night. As Charlotte saw him approach, she backed against the wall, certain he was looking for Nancy. She was shocked when instead he asked her to dance. She had flushed with some new emotion, something she couldn't distinguish. She felt an urgent need to be found acceptable to a boy, any boy. The sudden sense that no other acceptance could quite matter rushed over her. And here now, she had at last been found acceptable. Why then did she feel such an odd sense of elation and agony at once? She did not refuse the offer, the astonishing gift of that languid boy. He was nonchalant, which Charlotte understood was his way of hiding his interest. He did not look at her once as they danced to "Sugar, Sugar." In her nervousness Charlotte felt her movements had grown stiff and spastic. She blushed, although it seemed Brad did not notice her, seemed in fact, determined to appear not to be with her at all. He was not fooling her with his mask of cool.

When after the dance he left her without saying a word, Charlotte watched as he crossed the floor and found Nancy again. Nancy was laughing as Brad bent to talk to her, his lips close against her ear. He looked deeply at Nancy as he had not looked at Charlotte, and a stab of something more vicious and vile than she'd ever felt in her life ran against Charlotte's mind. She hated Nancy then, hated her, her best friend, her familiar playmate, now a competitor, a thief.

On the way home after the dance, in the backseat of Charlotte's father's Chevy, Charlotte tried to keep the new hateful feelings at a distance, though they clutched at her like tiny sharp nailed hands, pulling at her skin. Pinching. Nancy had chattered on, flushed and excited by her success, oblivious, it seemed, to Charlotte's silence, Charlotte's mortification. Before she left, Nancy leaned into the car to say, and Charlotte couldn't believe the sweet voice in which it was said, "Can you believe Brad wanted to dance with me all night? I finally told him I wouldn't dance with him again until he'd danced with my best friend." She smiled at Charlotte. "I think he really likes me."

The car's heater felt oppressive, and as they drove away from Nancy's house, Charlotte tore at her scarf, pulled off her mittens. Her father watched her in the rearview mirror. When she caught his eye he said, "Not a fun evening?" Charlotte did not respond. What did he know?

Later, Charlotte would wish again and again to relive that moment, her father's question, his attempt at understanding. Of all the things in her life, she would wish she had responded to him that night, Valentine's Day, 1972.

The morning after the dance Charlotte had awakened late and come into the kitchen to find her mother sitting stiffly at the kitchen table. Charlotte took no particular notice as she poured herself a glass of orange juice and sat down across from her. The note was still there on the table, in her father's hand, "I've gone to a warmer climate," was all it said. Charlotte read it upside down and then turned the note toward her and read it again. "What's that mean?" she asked her mother after she'd read it a second time. Only then as she glanced up did Charlotte note her mother's tears.

"Oh, honey," was her mother's response, and Charlotte didn't know if her mother said it tenderly or with exasperation. He'd simply gone away, must have been planning it, Charlotte realized, even as he drove her and Nancy through the snowy streets after the dance the night before.

Had he meant to say goodbye to her? To slip her a forwarding address, a phone number? Had he meant to say, call if you need me, come if you need me, but been distracted from his intention by her mood that night? Did he have a suitcase in the trunk even then?

That was the story Charlotte told Russell, a story she had never told anyone before. Russell had looked at her across the assembly room table for a long time afterward, the very table still there now in the assembly room. He looked at Charlotte long enough to cause her alarm. What was he thinking? Finally, he quit what he was assembling—Charlotte remembered it yet, a large wooden plaque with a number of names etched in columns on a gold plate—and silently walked around the table to hug her. He never said a word about the story, not then, not in the seventeen years since, but without fail the roses arrived, bearing a new message every year. She had known from the first they were a gift from him, but Charlotte never understood if the roses were meant as a consolation to her, or as a reminder of what a jerk her father was to have left.

The snow kept falling through the morning, gathering and drifting against the curbs. At noon Charlotte sent Kevin and Helen home. They weren't being productive anyway, and she couldn't see keeping them when there would be no more customers. At 2:00 the owner called and told her to shut down early. Charlotte busied herself preparing to close the shop: lights out in the storeroom, she'd sweep tomorrow; invoices back in their file, the cash register totaled—easy enough today, not one sale.

Finland was the last place Charlotte would want to be right now. The thought of going someplace colder was horrible. Russell must really love this man. She hated to admit it, but she wasn't optimistic about things working out. Charlotte knew that she and Russell had different notions of what it meant for things to work out. They had different notions as well about what it meant to love someone. Charlotte was thinking about this when the bell on the door jangled. The typewriter repairman smiled. "What did I tell you about this weather?" His smiled seemed radiant.

"I sent the assemblers home a couple hours ago," Charlotte said, wondering why she said it.

"You'd best be getting there yourself. It's a bear driving out there."

Charlotte felt a strange lift, a fluttering. Why had he come back? Just to tell her this? Now that she thought back hadn't he seemed awfully interested in her earlier? All those questions.

"I'm leaving right now," she said. "The owner just gave me word to shut down."

"I'm glad I caught you then."

Here it was. Why else would he drive through the snow?

"I forgot to leave something when I was here earlier." He seemed to lower his voice mysteriously as he walked toward her to the counter. "I forgot to leave the bill this morning."

A smile went stiff on Charlotte's face. "You drove through the snow to leave this?"

"You're on my way home. No trouble." He turned to go. "You be careful driving home."

She followed the repairman to the door. As she watched him get into a newer model silver LaSabre, she locked the door and turned the sign from Open to Closed. On the seat beside him he no doubt had a box of chocolates or a bracelet wrapped for his wife or girl-friend. They'd have to cancel their plans for the evening, but they'd be together anyway, maybe light a fire, laugh at how the weather hadn't really got the better of them. Charlotte shivered and rubbed her bare arms as she watched the repairman drive away.

After Canaan

Later, Sophia understood her education had started with this simple phrase: "Would you like to help me with the cooking while we put up hay next week?" It was her mother-in-law, Elva, speaking. They had been eating Sunday dinner at Elva's house. Sophia had just married Elva's son Sammy a month earlier.

"I don't think so," Sophia had said. "I'm no cook. I'd only be in your way, but thanks for asking."

As Sophia spoke everyone at the table had stopped eating. They had looked slowly from Sophia to Elva, whom Sophia noticed had tightened her jaw; her eyes set with a flat, glassy expression. Sophia had looked at Sammy, who frowned and shook his head slightly. Sophia had shrugged, and to hide her discomfort took a bite of the green Jello on her plate. Peripherally, she sensed Elva's face relax then and with it everyone at the table, Sammy, his two brothers and two sisters, and his father Big Sam. Sammy was the oldest and the first to be married.

"What was that all about," Sophia had asked as they got in the truck to drive home. "You'd have thought I'd peed in the potatoes for all the tension at that table."

Sammy laughed and shook his head a little sadly. "There's a lot you don't understand yet."

"A lot I don't understand? She asked me a question. I answered her. I can't cook. I wasn't going to lie about it."

Sammy nodded. "I know what you were thinking. It's just that Mother is never asking a question. She's always giving an order." He chuckled softly. "It was almost worth it to see Mother's reaction. No one ever stands up to her."

"But I wasn't standing up to her. I have no interest in standing up to her."

"Oh, but you were."

Afterward, when Sophia told her parents about the scene at Sunday dinner, they blamed it on her childhood passivity.

"You were always a child content to go along for the ride, oblivious to the sights outside, passive and compliant." her mother said.

"What does Elva's reaction have to do with my passivity?"

"What you're mother is trying to say," her father said from the other line, "is that your situation, living in a ranching community, something for which you're obviously ill-suited, is a symptom of an enduring personality trait."

"I called you for comfort," Sophia said, "not for psychoanalysis."

"We're sorry, dear," her mother said. "We thought you were trying to understand why you were unhappy."

"I'm not unhappy; I'm confused."

Neither of her parents spoke for a minute. "Yes, I suppose you are," her father finally said. "I suppose there's no use placing blame at this stage."

"It's only natural, though, to look for something to blame," her mother said. This was the place in the conversation where Sophia knew it was pointless to continue.

After she hung up Sophia thought about what her parents had said. She didn't blame her passivity. She blamed Sammy Stone's tight blue jeans—Wranglers, barely worn, the leg wide enough at the bottom to accommodate his cowboy boots and tight enough at the top to give her a pretty good idea of what sort of piece he was packing. She had seen Sammy Stone in those jeans for the first time through the fog of Jim Beam and the smoke of a campfire their last month of college. At that time in her life Sophia had given up on the idea of ever finding a nice guy. The way she saw it, her choices ranged from gropers and whiners to the peculiar narcissism of nerds and geeks. The search for a nice guy looked bleak, and she had begun only half jokingly to explore her options in the single life—permanently single, as in dorm mothers and au pairs. She wasn't putting a lot of stock in her BA in elementary music education, not for the long haul anyway. Unlike most of her friends she hadn't really formulated much of a plan for the future.

Sammy's jeans got her attention first, they were all she could see sitting cross legged by the fire when he approached, but it was his smile that hooked her. Sincere, sweet, open. It was a smile to lay odds on. Sammy had been wearing a brown cowboy hat, and he had taken it off when Sophia looked up at him. He held the hat against his chest, over his heart, as he introduced himself. The sweetest and weirdest guy Sophia had ever met. She would later admit that Sammy had come along at her lowest point. She was stunned by him. She felt swept away by it all, and easily confused shock and gratitude with love at first sight.

Sophia only remembered snatches of that first night—more whiskey, what amounted to a wrestling match with Sammy in the back seat of his '74 Barracuda and a breakfast of pancakes and eggs during the still dark, early morning hours. In the hostile light of Perkins Sophia had the first real look at the man she thought she'd fallen in love with. Their sleepless night showed on his face—small dark circles under his eyes, and a grayish pallor beneath his skin, all of which contributed to his rugged good looks. His hair was dark blonde. He wore an impressive mustache a shade darker than his hair, and his thick eyebrows—the same color as his mustache—grew together above the bridge of his nose. His square jaw was heavily stubbled with a morning beard. One front tooth was slightly crooked in an otherwise perfect smile. Sophia liked that flaw enormously. It endeared Sammy to her, made him less intimidating as she realized she had fallen in love with the Marlboro Man.

At breakfast that morning, Sammy said things like, "Whoowie, that sure was quite a night we had," and "Jeepers, these eggs taste good." Sophia thought some of this was for show. She thought he was a wannabe cowboy. Kind of cute and kind of irritating all at once.

They thought they were in love, convinced they were part of an epic love story, a love story among love stories. After a few weeks on this high, during which they took final exams in a stupor and marched through graduation equally stupid, they eloped in Iowa on a Friday night the week after they graduated—Sammy with a degree in animal husbandry and Sophia in music education.

They honeymooned in Des Moines and took a meandering turd-town-tour of Iowa on their way back home to Nebraska. It rained the entire time. The rain only intensified the sense of their romance as destiny. Only as they reached Omaha did it hit them what they'd done and how little they knew about each other. The subject of their families, where they would live, or what they would do for money had not come up until then. As they crossed the Missouri into Omaha the dreary day and the gray skyline plunged them both into silent despair. They knew, though neither said anything, that they had made a mistake and now they would have to face the consequences, starting with calling their families. The thought of divorce did not enter Sophia's mind, and she felt sure Sammy didn't consider it either.

"I guess we better call the folks, huh?" Sammy had said, looking sheepish, looking suddenly like a ten-year-old as he mentioned his parents.

"The sooner the better," Sophia said, and decided she needed a coat of lipstick for the task. She pulled down the visor on her side with its foggy mirror and took out a tube of Brandywine Mist, which she negotiated and steadied into application position in the bouncing car. As she formed her mouth into an oval to apply the lipstick, Sammy looked across the seat at her with a frown. Sophia could sense the frown peripherally by the set of his head. She stopped what she was doing.

"What?" she asked and frowned back at him.

"Why are you gobbin' up your face with that stuff? All's we're gonna do is make a few phone calls."

Sophia hesitated a moment then returned to her task. She finished applying the lipstick then looked at Sammy and heard her mother's voice say, "First of all, I'm not gobbin' up my face," she said. "And secondly, I'd appreciate it if you didn't patronize me. You're not my father."

"That's for damn sure," Sammy said. "If I was your father you'd have turned out a helluva lot . . ." he seemed to search for a word, "kinder than you did," he finally said.

"Kinder? What does kind have to do with it? I'm kind."

The conversation quickly deteriorated into a fight they both regretted. It was in the spirit of this fight that they called their parents with the news of their marriage. Sophia's family's initial impression of Sammy, formed no doubt in good part by that tearful telephone conversation, was little better than it would have been had Sammy been the wild centaur Eurytus and Sophia the innocent Hippodame dragged off by her hair. Her father was a Classics professor. Sophia knew how he thought.

"But your music," was all her mother said. At this, Sophia had rolled her eyes and did not reply.

As for Sammy's parents, Sophia was a conniving manipulator who had tricked and trapped their son. They didn't say this in so many words, but it was the gist of their concern. They refused to believe Sophia wasn't pregnant. Sammy listened and nodded a lot while he was on the phone with them. They didn't ask to speak to Sophia.

Sophia's father was the one to raise the issue of income. He directed Sophia to put Sammy on the phone. It was then as she listened to Sammy's end of that conversation, Sophia learned that where they would live and what they would do had already been decided. Sammy's family owned land in western Nebraska, near a town called Canaan. It was her first realization that Sammy really was a cowboy.

"It's all been taken care of, sir. No need to worry, sir. She'll be well taken care of, sir," Sophia felt as though she'd been bought and sold as she listened.

Sammy had compromised and they rented a house in town rather than living on the ranch. Sammy's family had raised a ruckus, but Sammy, speaking for Sophia, had said she'd be bored silly on the ranch and when a chance came up she'd need to teach the school kids their music.

Sophia couldn't appreciate the extent of Sammy's compromise at first. Only as she watched him commute seven days a week to tend the large herd of cattle he and his family owned, could she understand the sacrifice he made for her. It was a large ranch—forty thousand acres—beginning eleven miles southwest of town. Sammy's family was what the folks in Canaan called "well situated."

Shortly after they were married, Sophia learned two important things about Canaan. The first came about after a casual comment she made about how everyone she met seemed to have the same last name.

"Almost everyone does have the same last name," Sammy said. "So what?"

She laughed. "You don't have to be so defensive. I was just making an observation."

Sammy didn't smile. "Suit yourself," he said.

"So are you all related or something?" Sophia asked. Until this moment, and Sammy's strange reticence, it hadn't occurred to her.

"Not everyone," Sammy said. "But most everyone." Sophia raised her eyebrows. She thought about pressing the issue, but Sammy's rigid expression made clear he was not interested in talking about it. So she kept to herself her opinion that the whole thing reeked of depravity.

Next, she learned about the schism in Canaan only by accident. Sammy worked long days on the ranch with Big Sam. To occupy herself, Sophia adopted the habit of taking long walks about town and into the surrounding countryside. The first week she lived in Canaan she noticed a large stand of lilac bushes bordering a well kept yard on the east side of town. The lilacs smelled so sweet in the early morning air that Sophia decided to pick a bouquet to carry with her as she walked.

Just as her hand touched a stem of blossoms, still wet with rain from the night before, a large man stepped out of the back door of the house. He wore faded overalls, only one strap hooked over a torn, white T-shirt, and an apron tied around his waist, the apron looking like a dishtowel for all it covered of his massive belly.

The man shook his finger at her. "Don't you know you're one of Obadiah's?" he said. "Keep yourself on your own side of town."

That evening when Sophia mentioned the incident to Sammy he was amused. The man, it turned out, was Clarence Stone, Sammy's distant cousin, whom everyone knew as Bip.

"Granddad Obadiah," Sammy explained, "my great-great-grandfather and his brother, Clinton Stone, came out here in 1873 from Illinois. They called the town Canaan because of the Promised Land in the Bible, but it was the Bible that caused the mess in the end. They were Episcopalian, built a church first thing after they got here. About a year later, Granddad Obadiah heard a traveling Baptist preacher and claimed he'd gotten religion. Granddad decided the Episcopalians were wrong in their thinking. He ended up calling them Episcolopians just to be ornery. He was convinced the Baptists had the secret to getting into heaven. By the time Granddad had finished his tirade against the Episcopalians half of the congregation left the church with him. They built a Baptist church across the street from the Episcopalian church—the same churches that are there today. Since then, there's been no peace between the two sides of the family, except now and then when someone marries across."

Sophia, who had never attended church, thought of Sunday mornings as a time to leisurely read the newspaper. Though Sammy wasn't a religious man himself, once they were married and living in Canaan, Sophia discovered church attendance was compulsory. It also turned out there was a tradition of homegrown Baptist ministers in Canaan. Riley Stone, Sammy's cousin, was the Baptist minister.

Riley Stone was a peculiar man. He was not quite 5′2″ tall. In his early thirties, his hair was already white. His face was florid, not just ruddy, but as Sammy described it, red as a baboon's ass. Riley—Pastor Stone— had a queer habit of rocking back and forth from his heels to the balls of his feet as he preached. He kept one hand in his suit pants pocket and gestured with his free hand, upon which he wore a large gold ring, a cross imprinted upon its face. He refused to wear the traditional church robes, said they were pretentious, but Sammy told Sophia it was because they made Riley look like a squatty blue mushroom.

Sophia left church after hearing the first of Riley's sermons with a form of motion sickness caused both by his rocking and his theological sophistry. By the following Sunday Sophia solved the problem by focusing her attention on the bottom of the large cross which hung suspended by a thin wire above and behind the pulpit. She easily tuned out Riley and daydreamed while looking attentive, a technique she'd perfected in educational methods classes at the university.

Since no one discussed Riley's sermons, Sophia began to assume everyone practiced a similar habit. That was, until another Sunday family dinner after she and Sammy had been married about six months.

"So, you don't like us much then," Elva said in the

middle of dinner that day. Sophia glanced around the table, wondering to whom she was speaking. "You," Elva said and pointed at Sophia. "You don't like us much."

"Excuse me," Sophia said.

"You aren't happy here. You aren't happy with Sammy." These weren't questions. She now understood that much about Elva.

"I don't understand," Sophia said softly. "Where are you getting these ideas?" Sophia still felt apologetic and shy around Elva, intimidated by her strong, brown, corded hands, and her severe high-cheeked beauty. Elva had the hard, lean body of someone who had spent a great deal of time on horseback. It was clear to Sophia, by then that it was Elva who ran the ranch, she who made the decisions, Big Sam complying like a hired hand.

She answered Sophia's question then. "You've been asked to join the Ladies' Aid down to the church and you just keep refusing."

"I'm sorry, but I haven't been asked," Sophia said.

"But you have."

"I don't even know what the Ladies' Aid is," Sophia said and that was the wrong thing to say.

Elva's face stiffened. "Riley says it every Sunday from the pulpit, says all the women're invited to join."

Sophia glanced quickly at Sammy who was no help as he wolfed down his mother's mashed potatoes and pretended not to notice what was happening.

"I just assumed he wasn't including me in that invitation," Sophia finally said. "I'm so new here and all."

Elva frowned, obviously impatient with Sophia's thickheadedness. "Who else would he be asking except you? You're the only one there who don't belong already."

The following week Sophia attended her first meeting of the Ladies' Aid. She was surprised when after the minutes of the previous meeting were read and all new business discussed—responsibilities in the coming month for communion, cleaning the church, and providing food for Mrs. Frank Stone's funeral dinner, who although still living, at ninety-four years old and hospitalized with a broken hip, was due to die any day—after all of these issues had been settled, several of the women shared poems they had written that month. They were inspirational poems.

When Sophia asked Elva about it later she learned that most of the women wrote at least a little poetry. It was such an important part of the group that the church cookbook, sold annually to raise funds, included not only favorite recipes but poems written the previous year as well.

At that first meeting one of the more prolific poets, Myra Stone, read a poem:

> We are all on the way,
> Of returning to sod,

But we're all in His hands,
The hands of God.

Except for His love,
The love of God,
We would have no will,
On to trod.

He gave His life,
The Son of God,
To save us from sin,
By His blood.

None of the women were rude to Sophia after that first meeting, but no one was particularly welcoming either, except Miss Clara. A diminutive woman, well into her eighties, Miss Clara dressed immaculately, her white hair tinged with a pink rinse, a confetti hairnet holding it neatly in place. She came to stand by Sophia's elbow after the meeting that day and said something very softly, too softly for Sophia to hear. Miss Clara was so tiny that Sophia, who gangled over her, had to bend down to hear as she might have bent toward a child. She leaned close enough to see the softness of the wrinkled skin on Miss Clara's face and to smell her face powder—sweet and chalky.

"Wasn't that a purty poem," Miss Clara said.

Pretty seemed like a strange word choice, but Sophia was so relieved to have someone to talk to she fairly gushed about the poem herself. She could see she had overwhelmed Miss Clara a little but could not seem to stop herself. In the course of her nervous chatter Sophia managed to invite herself to Miss Clara's house for coffee the next day.

"Great," Sophia said. "I'll be there at 2:00 then."

"Oh," Miss Clara said twisting her hanky. "Okay."

The next day Sophia arrived at Miss Clara's front door at 801 Mill Street. Miss Clara opened the door. Her hands fluttered about her face like parakeets let out of their cage. Sophia tried to overlook Miss Clara's hysterical hands and followed her into the kitchen, where she sat down without being asked at Miss Clara's pink enameled table in a pink vinyl chair. Her tiny house smelled like cedar and ammonia.

Miss Clara hesitated, moved to sit beside Sophia, then caught herself and said, "You were coming to coffee?"

"Coffee'd be great," Sophia said. Miss Clara smiled wanly, nodded, and walked to the kitchen counter. Once there, she opened and closed all the cupboard doors, ran the tap, took out a few pans, put them away again with a clatter, fiddled with the knobs of the stove without actually turning on the flame, and returned to turn on the water once more. By this time, Miss Clara had begun to mutter to herself. Sophia couldn't understand what she was saying, but it was clear she was in great distress. Finally, Sophia got up from her chair and went to stand beside her at the counter. She put her arm gently across Miss Clara's shoulders.

"The coffee was wonderful, Miss Clara."

Miss Clara sighed and nodded. "Oh, that's good," she said and turned her filmy blue eyes toward Sophia. Her mouth trembled.

Sophia met Sammy at the door that night to tell him what had happened.

He was not pleased. "Why'd you go over there anyway?" he asked.

"She was nice. I like old ladies."

"I like old ladies too," he said, "but I don't impose on them."

"Impose? I wasn't trying to impose."

"Well you did, dummy. Anybody'd have told you, if you'd asked, that Miss Clara isn't right."

"I didn't know I needed to ask permission before I went to visit someone," Sophia said.

"There are things you still have to figure out," Sammy said, frowning. His hair was matted where he'd worn his cowboy hat all day. His forehead was white while the bottom half of his face was tanned brown. He looked like a pinhead, Sophia thought.

Sammy relaxed a little then. He smiled and gently punched her shoulder. "Dummy," he said again. He said it like it was an endearment. Sophia bit her lip. She felt tears gather. At this, Sammy took her in his arms. She didn't care that he pressed her face close to his dusty, sweaty clothes. Later, he told her that Miss Clara's sister, Ona, had taken care of her and her house for years so Miss Clara could live on her own. Now that

Ona was getting older, Ona's two daughters helped out too.

When the Ladies' Aid printed their annual report in September that year, Sophia saw there had been a typo making the balance of their checking account $44,172.53. She laughed at the error, but the women looked at her—puzzled.

"It's not a typo," Millie Stone, the President, said.

"What?" Sophia said. Without stopping to think, she went on, "Why don't you give it away or something?"

"We do, dear," Millie said. "We give to the orphanage in San Vicente, Mexico, and to the Jenkins family in Kenya and we contribute to the general conference fund too."

Sophia sighed, frustrated. "I don't understand why you still have such a large balance, though. What's the point?"

After a brief silence, Phyllis Stone, Sammy's cousin finally said, "I agree with Sophia. We could afford to give away more than we do."

The older women were quiet for a while, until Rita, Sammy's aunt, moved they send something to the orphanage. "Something extra for Christmas," she said. The women agreed this was a good idea, a one time gift above their usual monthly commitment.

"I move we send $1,000," Phyllis said and looked at Sophia with bright eyes. She winked as though they were co-conspirators. The older women seemed cowed by this amount. They looked anxious. Phyllis later explained their hesitation to Sophia: it was the Great Depression. The older women tended to horde. They didn't want to be caught off guard again like they had been then.

After several minutes of silence, Viola Hansen seconded the motion. The group approved, and Sophia was left marveling. It was in that moment Sophia first understood how much her life had changed. Living in Canaan was never going to make sense, she guessed, and the logical thing to do was what she'd always done, go along for the ride. The Ladies' Aid gave Sophia the honor that day of drafting a letter to the orphanage on their behalf explaining their generous gift.

Despite the fact that Sophia remained an unbeliever, she was welcomed into the Ladies' Aid. The question of faith simply never came up. Sophia guessed groups of people were a lot like music. Their common language could be learned like the notes and rhythms of a song. As long as one stayed in the designated key and kept the right rhythm it was easy to blend in. This was the ticket to getting along with Elva, too, Sophia concluded. All it would take was a little practice.

And with Sammy as well. During busy seasons on the ranch, he comes to bed long after Sophia is asleep and leaves before morning. He wakes her now and then in the night, and she teases him that he is playing Cupid to her Psyche. She sees how, with a little imagination, they can still think of themselves as part of a great love story.

Shortly after her first anniversary, Sophia started a tradition that she has maintained through the years. One night each spring she leaves the house. She walks quickly, keeping to the quietest streets. Occasionally a dog barks but otherwise she is unnoticed as she makes her way to the east side of town, to the lilac bushes bordering Bip's yard, and there, in the cool, dark air she takes a stem of blossoms. Only one, just in case Bip is watching from the darkened windows.

The Sensitive Man

Cliff Adamson learned his new girlfriend, Heather Lange, was being followed by a man on a Harley two weeks into their relationship. Had she said it was a Harley? Surely it had to have been a Harley, no Goldwing, no Japanese rice-burner would do to describe his horror at her description of the stalker, but he honestly didn't think she had said it was a Harley, didn't think, and he hated to admit this prejudice in himself, she'd really know the difference. The Harley, he guessed, had been his invention, his contribution to the story.

Heather told him about the motorcycle man after dinner at his house: candles, wine, linguine with creamy Gorgonzola. While Cliff had cleared off the table, insisting she rest, Heather wandered to the front window, a glass of white wine in her hand, and Cliff looked up to see her standing there, her elegant form against the sheer curtain. It stopped him short, seeing her like that, a grace he hadn't noticed before, and he supposed he fell in love right then. Love seemed a risky venture after leaving a twenty-odd year marriage only a month before. He had children, after all, not much younger than Heather. But he decided to put away any feelings of guilt or inappropriateness and go for it. He remembered distinctly thinking those words, *go for it,* so contrary to what he might normally have said. As Cliff sliced the cheesecake he thought about how suitable it was to alter his language to mirror the alteration of his life. Those changes shouldn't and couldn't go unmarked.

It was then, as he returned to the living room to ask Heather if she'd like coffee with the cheesecake, though he already knew her well enough to know she would say "only if it's decaf," for which he was prepared, he noticed the change in her. He never did ask the question, for as he entered the room, he saw how the graceful form he'd just fallen in love with had stiffened. Whatever had happened to change Heather's posture had changed the feeling in the room, too.

"What's wrong, Heather?" he asked.

She turned to him then, trembling so he took her glass from her. Pale, so he led her straight to a chair. And again, "What is it?"

Heather swallowed hard. "I thought maybe he'd gone away," she said and ran her hand distractedly to her neck, fingers picking lightly at her collarbone.

"Who?" Cliff said.

"The man on the motorcycle." At this, Cliff went to the window and looked into the dark street.

He searched through the gloom for a motorcycle—thinking for a little while it was there, behind a car at the far end of the street.

"Just now?" he asked then.

"Yes," she said. And he looked again, craning to look as far as he could both directions, his forehead pressed against the cold window; it was winter, early January.

"Well, he seems to be gone now."

"Is he?" Heather said, her tone of voice strange, eager, almost a whisper.

"Who is he?" Cliff knelt beside Heather where she sat in the chair. Her face was still pale in the glow of the candles. He had heard criticism of the tendency in men to desire weakness and illness in women; Cliff had heard it a few times from his wife, a healthy, strapping woman, but until tonight he had not seen it in himself. Tonight, though, he had to admit he desired Heather more because of her drawn appearance, and the fear too, how erotic. This wasn't something Cliff liked knowing about himself, but there it was. All the while he had been gently squeezing Heather's hand, telling her everything would be all right, though he still did not know exactly what was wrong.

Once she settled down and felt well enough in fact to eat a piece of his cheesecake—remarking again, as she had been all evening, what a wonderful cook he was, her comments always contrasted with some self-deprecatory remark about how she couldn't cook, how she was a downright putz in the kitchen—Heather told him about the man on the motorcycle, how for years he had been following her. She didn't know the man, had no idea who he was, couldn't even say for sure if she'd recognize him without the motorcycle. For all she knew, he was an acquaintance, someone she saw every day. He wore a silver helmet so she couldn't see his face, but she always recognized him because of that same silver helmet, the black motorcycle, and the way his body looked straddling the machine. She shivered when she said that, and went on to tell Cliff how sometimes the man called her at work, at her house.

"What does he say?" Cliff asked pulling a footstool close to the chair, his knees pained from kneeling so long.

Heather shrugged. "Different things."

"Like what? Does he threaten you? Does he make . . . you know, innuendos?" Heather laughed, and her laughter surprised him. She was always teasing him about being delicate, using polite language. She found it old-fashioned and without her saying it, he guessed, uptight, too.

"I honestly don't know," Heather said, still smiling. It bothered Cliff, that lingering smile while recalling what could only be seen as threatening phone calls from a stalker, no matter what he was saying. "I've probably blocked it from my mind," she continued. "As soon as I hear his voice, I just freeze up." She squeezed Cliff's hand hard.

"Yes, I saw that—just now at the window."

Heather nodded. "When he's around I feel trapped. I feel paralyzed."

"What do the police say?"

"What can they say? He hasn't done anything. I don't even call them anymore. I used to. They watched my house for a while, but he's too smart. He didn't show up while they were around, of course." Heather shook her head with a frown. Her frown was very reassuring to Cliff, a trace of anger toward the police. "The thing is, I thought he'd gone away. I haven't seen or heard from him for several months now." She looked at Cliff, held his gaze, her eyes softening. "It's you. It's because of you he's back. He must have been watching all along, knew about you, must have followed me here tonight."

This revelation created a queer excitement in Cliff; it tingled down his extremities. The feeling, not unpleasant, was one he experienced with the news of a terrible storm, an auto accident, a quickening he recognized as the prelude to something dramatic, possibly dangerous. His part in Heather's story gave him a significance in her life and she in his. He saw it in one brilliant moment. If the motorcycle man's intention had been to separate them, to intimidate or frighten Cliff away, the plan had backfired. They would cling to one another in a new way now. They had suffered something together.

Understandably, Heather was afraid to go home

that night, and even had she not been he would have insisted she stay.

"If it's too soon," Cliff said, "if you'd prefer, I can make up a bed on the couch."

Heather laughed. "Your bed's cool."

It seemed fitting to Cliff that that night was the first time they made love, and he couldn't lie to himself. The experience was heightened, made urgent by the danger of the motorcycle man. He made love to Heather in a proprietary way, as though she were a fragile possession, held her close through the fitful night as though to reassure himself she was still there and safe. The things Cliff had anticipated as challenges to their relationship—the caustic sarcasm of his estranged wife, the disapproval of his colleagues at the office, the disgust of his children—all paled in light of this new threat.

In the weeks following, there were numerous sightings of the motorcycle man: outside Heather's downtown office building she saw him several times, once, with a chilling casualness innocently riding through traffic; she saw him outside her apartment building both morning and night, though never in any sort of detectable pattern. She saw him less frequently near Cliff's apartment. And the man called too: at her office, at her apartment, hanging up if he got her answering machine. Cliff had heard the hang up calls himself, a whole tape of them, insidious for their peculiar silent threat.

At first Cliff had felt Heather shouldn't be alone at

night, not now with so many more sightings of the stalker. For a while, he stayed at Heather's apartment, which seemed to keep the man away, and for a few weeks Heather stayed with Cliff with similar good results, but they eventually had to agree their relationship was too new to withstand being together all the time. Cliff had discovered Heather's inadequacies in the kitchen extended to her sense of cleanliness in general, and he could not relax at Heather's place. Clothes strewn over furniture, dishes left in the sink, the bathroom fixtures gray with grime; the untidiness made him nervous, and he couldn't help feeling that the way she lived was at odds with her appearance. When she was staying with him, she did not abandon her bad habits but quickly cluttered his place as well. Cliff found himself thinking at one point she was more than just a putz in the kitchen, then caught himself, upbraided himself for his harshness toward this young woman in crisis. After all, why did she need to be neat?

Cliff was trying to be sensitive, trying to live down something his wife had said before he left, that no one could accuse him of being sensitive. Heather was his chance to prove Vivian wrong. And hadn't he handled himself admirably through this whole stalking ordeal? Heather had told him repeatedly how grateful she was for his support. There, she even said it, "his sensitivity."

On a clear day in April, after they'd been seeing one another for a few months, Heather called Cliff's office, as she had so often before, and Cliff recognized by the now familiar tautness in her voice, the signal she had had some sort of encounter with the motorcycle man. Her call had interrupted his reading of an important deposition. That was how he explained the impatience he felt. Also, he had not slept well the night before after having been awakened by a frantic call from her. It was some meaningless state holiday, and she had the day off while he, a lawyer, didn't. Cliff felt a moment of disgust as he suddenly pictured Heather still in her worn terry cloth robe, her hair slightly matted from sleep. He felt as well a sliver of jealousy. "He's here again, Cliff," she said. "His helmet is shining in the sun." Her voice lowered to a whisper then, as though she thought the man might be able to hear her. "Oh my god, he's looking at my window. He's looking straight at me." Cliff suddenly pictured Heather crouching, peeping out the window as he listened to her go on to describe her fears about what the motorcycle man might possibly be thinking or doing. He listened with a detachment that surprised and frightened him, and though he believed Heather's fear was real, he felt it was weightless, ungrounded. Had he wanted to, he knew he could formulate questions to throw into light how preposterous her story was, the biggest one being, "Why are you the only one who ever sees this guy?" He felt as though he had caught her in some contradiction, and sensing his distance, Heather talked all the more, even asking once with genuine hurt, "Don't you believe me, Cliff?"

"Of course I believe you, darling," he said. The small lie he felt was so essential to the fabric of an intimate relationship, but as soon as he hung up the phone, continuing in the vein of his disbelief, he made some excuse to leave the office and drove straight to her street where he parked out of view from her window. For an hour, he stayed there in the warm April sunshine listening to the twittering of the birds and the shouts of small children playing on the sidewalk. In that hour he saw nothing, most of all, he felt nothing.

Cliff was convinced if there was a stalker, if the stalker had been anywhere in the vicinity of Heather's apartment in the recent past, he would have sensed him. He would have felt that keen awareness he had as a young man while hunting, the charge between the hunter and the hunted, the electricity that more often than not gave away the deer or the wild turkey before even the sharpest eyes could find the animal through the camouflage of the woods. There was no evidence of a motorcycle man. Cliff had learned to watch people closely through depositions and cross examination, and there was something missing in Heather's story. Had there been a motorcycle man, he would have felt it in his bones.

He started his car then and pulled around the corner to park in front of Heather's apartment building. As soon as he rang her bell she breathlessly pulled him inside. She was still in her old robe as he had earlier pictured it while they were talking on the telephone.

"Oh, Cliff, he was just here," she said. "He left just a minute ago. I'm so glad to see you."

Cliff's intention had been to confront Heather with what he knew, and what better time than now when she had so clearly been caught in her deception, but standing in her apartment and looking into her distressed eyes, he did a funny thing. He felt himself do it too, like switching the channels on a television, he recast the scene. To stay with a woman he loved, he willed himself to a kind of forgetfulness to keep . . . what was it? Peace? No, rather to keep safe in what he believed his life should be, a life which included Heather. He wondered in that moment about his wife. Had Vivian switched channels, too, thinking of him during their marriage as a better man than he was? Was what he considered Vivian's new-found vindictiveness since he had left only evidence of his fall from her grace? Without the habit of love, and what was this channel switching if it wasn't love to some degree, did she no longer need to cast him as better than he was?

A few nights later, he sat on Heather's couch after work and listened as she wondered aloud if her life would ever be normal. They were eating her version of dinner—saltines and American cheese, sliced apples, and pimento-stuffed olives on paper plates that kept buckling. Outside a soft, persistent spring rain tapped against the windows.

"I just don't understand why it happened to me,"

she said, near tears. "Maybe if I understood who the man was, I could make sense of things, but not knowing him is driving me crazy." Heather looked at Cliff in a beseeching way, and he believed her concern was justified. "Did I do something to deserve this? Is he someone I mistreated in the past?" She sucked the pimento from an olive, chewed it distractedly for a moment, and went on. "Those unanswered questions get to me sometimes. And it's not fair to other people in my life. After a while people always begin to doubt he exists. I think they find it exhausting to be around someone who lives in constant fear like I've had to. It's hard to comprehend. People want to think it can't happen to them," she said matter-of-factly. "They like to make it the victim's fault, so they can protect themselves, they think." By her account, she had suffered terribly for their disbelief. She wondered how many of the men she was involved with had left her finally, though they denied it always, because of the motorcycle man.

"Perhaps it wasn't that they didn't believe you, darling, but that they did believe you and they lacked the maturity to handle a situation in which they felt so out of control."

"What a sweet thing to say," Heather said. They had been sitting together on the couch while eating, and she tipped her head onto his shoulder, reminding Cliff disconcertingly for a moment of his youngest daughter, adding, "You always know the right thing to say." She took his paper plate from him and set it on the floor, her fingers finding the buttons of his shirt, her mouth against the bare skin of his chest, moving down his torso until all thoughts of his daughter disappeared.

Cliff felt buoyant when he returned to his apartment later that night. He hadn't been aware that he'd been struggling to breathe earlier until he now felt himself breathing easily. He had to admit he had been relieved when Heather had not wanted to come home with him, for though it seemed like a strange impulse, he wanted to clean his apartment. While he cleaned he understood two things: he had been spoiled in his marriage, and Vivian had been acting out, her cleaning a cathartic, symbolic purging of her anger toward him, toward the whole family perhaps. The semi-violent motions of scrubbing the toilet or running the vacuum brought about a release of frustrations Cliff hadn't wanted to admit. The motorcycle man was at the heart of it. That much he understood. But he was amazed to discover the extent of his resentment toward Heather, the ways he felt she had controlled his days, calling his office near hysteria, staying at his apartment, asking him to go to hers, waking him in the middle of the night because she was afraid. Even then Cliff knew it wasn't the specifics he resented. Like the others in her past, and a foggy past it was now as he thought about it, filled with vague people who did not properly appreciate her and impeded her progress, he too doubted her story of the motorcycle man. Although he had tried to overcome it, Cliff kept reliving that time a few days before when he had watched outside her apartment. Despite his best effort to deny his loss of trust, thinking it a lapse into insensitivity, he doubted. Why did this chill him so? He saw then clearly all the ways his life had been altered by his belief in the motorcycle man, the ways he had perceived Heather differently through the threat of that danger.

As he dusted end tables, straightened the shelves in the medicine cabinet, scrubbed the kitchen floor, Cliff replayed the weeks he had been with Heather. He watched the reel of memories critically, and this time willed himself not to recast anything, not to deny the evidence. How had he let himself be so deceived? She had seemed like such a strong, put-together young woman the first time he met her. Cliff remembered then what had struck him when they first met, a specific mannerism: the way she pushed her hair away from her face, a gesture both vulnerable and confident. Even now, recalling that mannerism, Cliff felt a softening toward her. He felt a dual urge to protect her and to undertake some enterprise with her. She would make a great witness, he decided. So sincere and sweet, so convinced of her own delusions.

The next day, Cliff still felt vengeful enough that he decided to enact a plan he had imagined the night before as he had changed his sheets. He carefully messed up his hair. He tied his trench coat at an odd disheveled angle. Still, in the mirror he saw that he was not yet convincing, so he began to picture what he was about to tell Heather. Like an actor rehearsing for a part, he made himself believe a story and in so doing he noticed that his breathing had become shallow, his face flushed, his heart pounded heavily in his chest.

Later, as he stood in Heather's living room, he was surprised at how thoroughly he had managed to convince himself, how agitated he felt.

"What's the matter, Cliff?" Heather said the moment she opened the door.

Cliff paced about her living room, too anxious to sit down. "I saw him," he blurted breathlessly.

Heather balked. She seemed cautious. "The stalker? You're sure it was him?"

"It was him. Who else would it be?" Cliff gestured toward the street. "I came earlier today, just to watch." He looked at Heather who nodded slowly. "And I saw the sonuvabitch parked in front of your building casual as you please." Cliff stopped pacing then and grabbed Heather's hands in his. "I couldn't help myself. You can't imagine how enraged I felt seeing him sitting there so cocky. I thought to myself, 'you're dead, asshole.'" Cliff dropped Heather's hands. He noted the puzzled looked on her face.

"Dead?" she said. "What do you mean?"

Cliff had begun to pace again, but he stopped now. "I meant it. I've killed him, Heather." He triumphantly crossed the room to embrace her. "You don't have to be afraid anymore." Heather did not return his embrace.

"You've killed someone?" she said when he pulled away from her.

"Not *someone*—the motorcycle man." He walked to the window and looked out. "No one will ever know. It was perfect. I drove up behind the motorcycle, kept inching closer and closer until he noticed and looked at me. Then I revved my engine. He got the idea then and left. That's what I'd wanted, of course, so I followed him. I kept tight on his tail through town, and I can't tell you, darling, how great it was to see that he was afraid, just like he'd made you afraid all these years." Cliff glanced at Heather with a smile before turning back to the window.

Heather did not respond at first, and Cliff was silent. "Go on," Heather said. She seemed put out with him.

"Like I said, it was perfect. He headed out of town on a gravel road. I know that road. I followed him, menaced him. He was terrified. I could see that. When we came to small bridge over an embankment, I sped up so I was right beside him. He looked at me then and I looked straight into that asshole's eyes before I ran him off the bridge."

"You killed him," Heather said.

Cliff turned and smiled at her. "Technically, I didn't do anything. He died in a motorcycle accident. They aren't very safe, you know."

"But you're sure he's dead?"

"Oh, I'm sure of that. I went down the embankment to check." Cliff pointed to the mud on his shoes. "He's dead all right. The motorcycle man will never bother you again."

Heather had gone pale. Cliff knew what she was thinking. She wanted to call his bluff but she couldn't, not without revealing her own past deception.

"Why aren't you happy, darling?" Cliff took her hands again. "You're free now. Aren't you happy?"

Heather frowned and then forced a smile. "Yes, I guess I should be." She was quiet.

"You seem tired," Cliff said.

"I am." Heather's weak smile had disappeared.

Cliff left then. They made no plans for the evening, and he felt certain now that this would be the end for them. It was the simple way to end the relationship, to be finished with a troubled, needy woman. He was proud of his performance, and he couldn't help but smile at himself in the rearview mirror as he pulled away from Heather's apartment building.

That evening his phone rang several times. Knowing it was Heather he did not pick up, nor did she leave any messages. The next evening he came home from work to find an entire tape full of hang up calls. Cliff understood then he would have to pay for his breach with Heather in this way, that she would continue to call until she met someone new. She was young, though, and not unattractive, and he knew she would soon replace him.

Dill

The bell above the door jangled and I looked up from behind the counter. "Evening, Buss."

"Evening, Dill." I work at Decker's, an all night convenience store, on the night shift. Some people think it's a dangerous job for a woman, but most of the people who come in here are regulars, and I've gotten to know them all. Whenever management offers me a day position I turn them down. I'd miss seeing the regular night folks. Everyone around here calls me Dill because of something that happened to me about five years ago when I first started this job. One night this guy I'd never seen before came in. I noticed him browsing for a long time through the canned foods. When he finally brought a jar of dill pickles to the front, he laid them down on the counter along with a piece of his anatomy. Without stopping to think, I picked up the jar of pickles and brought it down hard on him. I expected him to howl, but I didn't expect him to pass out. When I leaned over the counter to see what he was doing down there it looked at first like he might be dead. That's when I called the ambulance.

Buss put two packs of Lucky Strikes on the counter and pointed to a powdered sugar doughnut under a glass cover by the register. I got the doughnut for him and took his money, all in change.

"I seen your friend the other day," he said.

"Oh yeah. Who you talking about?"

"Nora."

"You mean you thought you saw Nora."

"Yes. I mean, no," Buss said.

I smiled. "So did she say what she's doing back here?" I asked.

Buss shrugged. "Can't say. She didn't even seem to know herself."

"Now what do you mean by that?"

"I said hello to her and she looked at me funny, like she didn't know who I was."

I laughed. "Buss, you goof ball. That's because it wasn't her. It was someone who looked like Nora. Nora's in Denver. I know that for sure."

Buss shook his head. "No. It was her. She looked bad though. Worse than when she left, but I know it was her 'cause of the scar across her nose where she took it in the alley that time. And I'm not a goof ball."

"Okay, you're right. You're not a goof ball."

"That's okay."

"It doesn't make sense that she hasn't come in here if she's back."

Buss bit into his doughnut and then started to talk, spraying powdered sugar and crumbs all over me. "Didn't your mother teach you any manners?" I said. "God, sometimes you act like a goat."

I noticed a rib of pain shoot behind Buss's eyes, then he grinned and covered his mouth while he finished chewing. "Like I said," he finally went on. "She didn't seem to know herself."

I shrugged. "Maybe you're right. I don't know, Buss. Why don't you ask around and find out if anyone else has seen her."

"Sure thing. See ya round, Dill." He paused in front of the door. "Do you really mean all them mean things you say to me?" he said.

"Course not, Buss. It's just my way."

Buss grinned again. "I thought so."

"Hey!" I shouted after him. "If you see Newton around send him in, would you?" Buss nodded from outside the door and walked away.

Newton's a hard guy to figure. Some people say he's a genius and others say he put his mind away for safe keeping and forgot where he hid it. I'm not so sure they aren't both right. He's always talking about this research he's doing, trying to reconcile the theory of relativity with some kind of quantum something— nonsense I don't know anything about. He gets so exasperated with people for not understanding him, though, that I fake like I can understand. I nod a lot and try to think of fairly intelligent questions now and then. I don't think he's really fooled by my act, but he talks to me anyway.

He has another theory that I know is crazy. He says he's invented an x-ray gun so small no one else can see it, and when he shoots it at people he can see into their souls and can tell which ones are saved and which ones aren't. In spite of his nonsense I wanted Newton's opinion about whether he thought Nora was around or not. He always seemed to know everything that was going down in the neighborhood.

Buss' story about Nora seemed unlikely except for the scar. There wasn't any way somebody else could have a scar like that. Nora'd gotten it in the face with a broken bottle one night in an alley. Nobody knew what she'd been doing in the alley alone in the first place, but we all figured something even worse had probably happened than getting her face carved up. It had been around that time I noticed that Nora was changing.

Nora and I met when I first started working at this place. We were both students back then. I was pretending to be a business major at the university for the sake of my mother. Nora was in elementary education. She used to come by at night when she needed a study break and we'd shoot the breeze or study together. Mainly we'd shoot the breeze. Nora dropped out of school after the first year. I hung in there another semester. I never really understood everything going on with her because I was having enough of my own bad times then, but somehow we got to be friends.

Nora was a beautiful woman. She had incredible, long, auburn hair, but after she got cut in the alley she quit taking care of herself. I figured her hair might be a hindrance so I asked her once if she had ever thought about cutting it off. When I asked that, she got this scared look on her face and put both hands against her head. "No!" she had said, her voice sounding like a little kid's, like she was begging me not to hurt her.

I just laughed. "Hey, it's all right. I was just asking to be asking, that's all." Nora didn't bring her hands down for a long time. That spooked me a little. She started doing other weird things, like always wearing a coat and hat even in the summertime, and we'd notice her talking angrily to herself. I didn't say anything about it to her because I figured she had her reasons for doing those things, and that if something was bugging her she'd work it out for herself.

Next thing any of us knew, though, her brother, Delbert, had been given some sort of guardianship over her and she'd gone to live with him in Denver.

"How ya doing, Dill?"

I looked up from where I sat on the floor dusting cans on the bottom shelf. I must have been pretty deep in thought not to have noticed the bell ring as Milcie came in. "Buss said you were wondering if anybody'd seen Nora around."

I nodded. She ran her fingers through her hair. She kept it short and greased back like a man's. "Well, I haven't seen her." She watched me work for awhile. "But you know Buss gets confused," she said then. I shrugged and she went on. "That Nora. I never liked her much. Too fragile. You couldn't talk to her at all."

"You have a right to your opinion," I said and stood up taking the dust rag I'd been using to a basket in the back room. When I came back Milcie was standing near the counter.

"Can I get you something, Milcie?"

"Not really. How come you liked Nora so much anyway?"

"How come I like anybody?"

"That's no answer."

I sighed. "Who knows. I don't know why you're asking."

"I just came in to tell you I haven't seen her."

I nodded. "Thanks."

"Sure."

After Milcie left I started feeling tired. Around 3:00 a.m. is the hardest time for me. I got myself a cup of coffee and sat down behind the counter with a copy of *Rolling Stone*. I had gotten pretty well into an article about the hex on Led Zeppelin when Newton walked in. His breath came in little gasps. He pushed his glasses up and looked around. Still not seeing me, I waved to him.

"Over here, Newton."

"Oh, yes. Buss told me there was an emergency. I've come as quickly as I could."

I rolled my eyes. "Buss was wrong. You want a cup of coffee?"

"I believe I would," he said and sat down on the chair I drug over beside mine. It's against the rules to allow customers behind the counter, but since none of the managers ever check on the night shift I take a few liberties.

"Buss exaggerated. There's no emergency," I said again. I told Newton then about Buss thinking he'd seen Nora and asked his opinion on the whole thing. Newton's forehead wrinkled and he stared for a long time into his coffee as though it were somehow going to reveal the truth of the matter. Finally he lifted his head and pushed his glasses up again.

"This is quite a mystery, isn't it?"

"I don't know that it's anything."

"Has anyone else seen Nora to verify Buss's story?"

I smiled as I shook my head. "No one except Milcie has come in tonight and she hasn't seen her."

Newton nodded. "Why don't we wait around a bit and see if anything turns up. I'll tell you right now, I believe Buss. We just need to think a while to know what to do next. The reasonable steps will be seen as time unfolds."

I smiled again. "I'm glad you're here, Newton."

The night seemed long, waiting until my shift ended. I felt restless and kept walking to the window and staring out at the darkness, then pacing back again to the freezer section at the back of the store. I remembered nights when Nora and I would sit behind the counter and eat candy bars and laugh. I couldn't remember what we'd found so funny. I couldn't remember either when those good times had stopped. Milcie had asked why I liked Nora. I knew why, I just didn't want to talk about it with Milcie. I liked Nora because I felt comfortable with her, because we didn't always have to talk to know what the other was thinking. Like I said, the good times, the laughing, easy times ended, but no matter what, we had been friends.

Buss came in again near the end of my shift. It had gotten cold in the night and when he opened the door it brought in a gust of cold air.

"Shut the door, quick," I said.

"I got news!" he said. Newton, who'd fallen asleep in the chair behind the counter, his head resting against the wall, woke up when Buss came in. We both waited to hear Buss's news.

When he said nothing Newton finally said, "Go ahead."

"Nobody I've talked to has seen Nora, but old Tiggums said there was some noise about a new woman around. He said from what he'd heard it sounded like Nora."

I glanced at Newton and raised my eyebrows. "What do you think?"

"I think it's a positive step."

I shrugged.

"You need to sleep now," Newton said. "Your shift is almost over. We'll think about it later."

"We're probably making a big deal over nothing," I said. "Besides, if Nora wants to see us, she knows where we are."

Newton nodded slowly. "I see what you mean," he said. He scratched his nose and then looked at me over his glasses. "You work tomorrow night?"

"No."

"Good. Maybe we can start a search of our own."

Buss looked from Newton to me and back again. "You're being pretty serious about all of this, huh? You think Nora's in trouble?"

"Goddamn you, Buss," I said. I was feeling pretty strung out by this time of the morning. "You come in here and get me all worked up, telling me Nora's in town and she looks bad and she doesn't seem to know herself, and now you're asking if I think she's in trouble. The question is, Buss, did you tell me the truth before or were you just talking to hear yourself talk? If we've got an old friend in the kind of shape you told me about we've got a friend in trouble, and if you've exaggerated and worried me for nothing you're in deep shit."

Buss swallowed hard and looked away briefly, then back again. "Now you're getting me all confused, Dill, when you start yelling and getting so mad."

I took a deep breath and spoke softly. "Okay, Buss. Again, did you see what you said you saw or were you just making conversation?"

"No, sir, I wasn't. I know what I seen. I seen Nora just like I told you I seen her."

I nodded. "That's all I wanted to hear, Buss."

"It was her. I know it," he mumbled and ran his hand through his hair.

When I get off work the rest of the world is waking up—ladies still in their robes and slippers taking little dogs out for their morning leak, paperboys with empty bags going home to get ready for school, delivery men loading their trucks, big dogs barking and birds twittering. I like to watch all the activity, to be a spectator and all the time know I don't have to be a part of it, getting up, putting on makeup, fussing with hair, stuffing myself into tight dresses and nylons and high heels. I did that for a while and I don't miss one day of it.

Now when I go home I kick off my tennis shoes and sit down to read the paper or watch a little TV. But mostly I don't miss not knowing too much about what's going on in the world. It just keeps happening no matter how much I worry about it. If I were a bit braver, and if it wouldn't drive my mother completely over the edge, I'd try to find a place to live that was real isolated, far away from Lincoln.

I got my mail before I went upstairs. There was a letter from my mother. For some reason I didn't want to hear from home just then and laid the unopened letter on my kitchen table while I fixed myself something to eat.

I had introduced Craig to Nora, not trying to be a matchmaker, just because we ran into him one day and I felt obligated to be nice and introduce them. I knew he was jerk, but not in any surprising way. He was just a jerk the way most nineteen-year-old boys who are handsome and talented are jerks, just thinking with his glands is all. Nora went crazy over him, though. They started seeing each other, and that's when things started getting weird with her. Nora quit thinking for herself, quit having her own opinions or feelings, quit laughing over the things she'd found funny before. She started to want whatever Craig wanted. She was nervous all the time about not being or feeling or thinking what he would want her to.

I've never been in love, and the older I get the more I think it's not a good idea to lose your head like that over someone. At first, when things weren't going well between Nora and Craig, she'd come to the store and we'd talk all night. She'd talk on and on, her eyes vacant. She never said anything much about Craig leaving her, but I could tell she didn't want to be alone right then. It was fine with me, gave me someone to talk to to pass the time. We'd work the crossword puzzle, or take all the surveys in the women's magazines, or she'd help me restock the shelves, or clean. I knew she was in trouble even back then. I watched her get sicker and sicker, but I didn't know what to do. I was afraid.

She got kicked out of her apartment for not paying rent, and because of complaints from neighbors, though she never told me what those complaints were. She lost her job and quit school. Her brother Delbert sent money each month for awhile, but she still couldn't seem to get things together. Some girls she knew let her live with them for a few weeks, but that didn't work out either. Eventually, the store became her home. She'd come in and I'd let her sleep in the back room every night I was working. I was risking my job to do that, but I felt it was the only thing I could do. For some reason I didn't want to ask her to live with me.

And then she said she was leaving and didn't tell me where she was going, except to live with her brother in Denver. I never heard from her again. That was two years ago.

Remembering all of this made me mad. I hadn't let myself think about it for a long time. After I cried for awhile and hit the wall a few times I felt tired and laid down. I wanted to sleep, but I kept thinking about Nora, worrying, feeling like there was something I should have done for her a long time ago and hadn't.

I tried to make myself feel better by reminding myself that I couldn't change things, and Nora was going to get sick whether I was a certain way or not. I said before that I've never been in love. That isn't exactly true. I loved Nora. She never knew it of course, wouldn't have understood it if she had known. I'm not sure I understand it myself. I don't think I loved her the way she loved Craig, but I would have done anything to make her happy. I thought about her all the time, and just knowing her made me feel good. I didn't care that she started not taking care of herself and not smelling so good. I didn't care that she couldn't really be a friend anymore because she was so strung out. Once in a while I'd make a suggestion, hint that she could clean up at my apartment if she wanted to, but she refused me, and that was okay too.

The thing that happened in the alley, I suppose that was when I really understood that she was never going to be the same again. I never said anything to the others, but I always suspected there really hadn't been an attacker, no stranger anyway. I think Nora hurt herself that night. She'd been saying things about how no one liked her except for her face. She thought her face was her enemy, and she wanted people to love her for who she was not how she looked. Crazy thing was, she couldn't understand that I did love her for who she was.

Nobody knows this but after Nora left for Denver, sometimes in the store at night I would think I heard her saying my name. I'd turn around getting my hopes all up, and the store would be empty and silent. I felt like someone had torn my guts out when she left. It sounds pretty weird. I don't know. But most of all I think Nora was special and that I just had to love her. I didn't have a choice. It's made me think that maybe we don't have any control over our lives, not really, and that maybe our decisions aren't decisions at all, but just what we were meant to do. All I know for sure is that I didn't want to care about anyone, couldn't have imagined caring before it happened, but somehow Nora got into my heart.

When I finally fell asleep I dreamt that I was in a room filled with people. It was a party, from all I could gather. There, in the crowd, I caught a glimpse of Nora—beautiful, like she had been when I first met her. She saw me too and looked away when our eyes met. I pushed through the crowd to where she had been and when I got there she was gone. Then I saw her again in another part of the room and fought my way across to her only to be frustrated again. This happened several times. I stopped then and thought and somehow I knew that she would be outside. Although it was snowing outside, I didn't take my coat with me. I didn't feel cold. Sure enough there was Nora sitting alone on a bench. She looked up at me when I came out and then looked away. I felt hurt by her rejection but sat down on a bench across from her anyway. I looked at her, drank her in, and leaned forward like I meant to touch her, but I didn't.

"Why are you avoiding me?" I asked finally. She didn't answer. I asked again and told her I had missed her, told her how I felt. I kept talking until after awhile someone from the party came out and suggested I go back inside. He said everyone was concerned about me sitting outside without a coat on talking to myself. When he said that I looked back to the bench where Nora had been and she was gone.

When I woke up I lay there on my bed not really thinking, just watching the way the sunlight came through the closed venetian blinds and tossed about on the ceiling.

As soon as I got up I had a strong urge to open the letter from my mother. News from home would be the same. My mother would talk about housework and who she had seen that week and where she had gone. There would be no surprises, no ambiguities.

I decided when Buss and Newton came that night I would tell them not to bother with the search. I knew there was no sense in us looking for Nora. Nora didn't want to be found.

The Blue Room

There is nothing blue in the room, only a particular cast of light, a tincture of blue. The air is very still beneath the high ceiling. A shaft of sun slants across the floor. It is day, late afternoon. Nothing stirs. The room is empty, and yet, a pulse in the air suggests that someone has just left in a hurry, upset perhaps. Something terrible may have happened only moments before. A phone call, an accident on the street, a child's scream upstairs. The air is still awash with a presence now absent; a shift in the atmosphere—bodies moving through space.

In the blue room is a piano, slightly out of tune, its finish cracked and peeling in places. The keys are ivory. None have been chipped, which is extraordinary given the piano's age, seventy-five years according to a serial plate just at the edge of the soundboard, and the fact that there are most likely children who have access to this piano. Sheets of music clutter the bench. The book propped on the music stand now is a children's book,

Alfred's Book One, though the Brahms on the bench suggests there is also in the house a player with greater facility.

Behind the piano hangs the photograph of a somber family dressed in high black collars, their hair coiled and coifed. Of course, the picture is black and white, so the question of color is irrelevant, and the assumption of coiled hair is not entirely sure. Who knows what hangs down the backs of these unsmiling people, what they are doing with their hidden hands. The men and women in the picture are good-looking, sharp eyed and clear skinned. All of them are slender except a very large, white-haired woman in the center, who is clearly the matriarch. She is splendid—by almost anyone's standards—splendid. There are no children, only youngish to middle-aged adults, though one supposes there are children somewhere who belong to these people.

In the photograph grown brothers and sisters surround aging parents, their mates and children absent. One wonders why. One wonders, too, what disorder has for this moment been restrained. What mucking about the photographer has had to squelch, perhaps the mother stepping in once again as if from the long past to shush these middle-aged children. After the photographer has indicated everyone can once again breathe normally, now that the shutter has been open long enough, what rush of breath? What eruption of laughter? What banter and tattling?

That day of the photograph, Sherman had been pinching Merle. Em did not join the rest of them in laughter. The youngest, this was strange, out of character, for in the picture it is clear she is the one seething with energy. But there is a sliver of sadness there in her eyes, that later the photograph reveals, something none of her brothers and sisters had seen that day, however quiet they remembered she had been. And her husband, Bertrand, also seemed unusually restrained, not what they expected from that rambunctious horse breaker.

Though petite, Emma built the house where she and Bertrand lived, and she broke horses alongside him. There was nothing spoiled about her, even with her glamorous good looks. She seemed not to notice her own appearance, and this was always to her credit. Only her mother watches today, the proverbial eyes in the back of her head, roving the space, alert, antennaed to trouble among her brood. Em denies anything is wrong, and even though her mother knows a lie when she hears one, she can't confront a grown daughter, especially not in the midst of the jocularity of the rest of this unrestrained and bountiful family—seven daughters and five sons—they've about killed her. The children.

And so has her quiet, hard-drinking Irish husband whose boxing days are long over, whose quick wit, equaled by his quick temper, saved them a myriad of troubles over the years with their suspicious Polish neighbors, but that's long ago in the past. A large barn, plenty of straw on the floor, a Polish band every Saturday night, a little hooch on the side if you're in the know, and they'll dance themselves silly. There'll be no trouble with the law as long as you share from your plenty and your expertise with the barley corn.

Those days are long past, everyone safely married away, with healthy dark-haired children skittering about like bugs so that their mothers were scolding up until the moment the photographer told the adults to quiet themselves. Even the children seemed to sense the charge and held themselves still, not breathing, the entire room suspended for one minute under the sway of the photographer from Sherman County.

Years later another photographer, Joanna. She'll marry Em's son Bruce. She is expert at getting the unexpected shot, the in-motion flight across the basketball floor, the boy getting bucked from a brahma bull. Her shots are entered digitally into a computer and acquired by newspapers across the country. She demonstrates now and then her ability to manipulate a photograph with the computer, moving a basketball in place of a boy's head. Her photographs win her awards, acclaim. She is the master sleuth, sly with the camera, so quick you don't know she's been in the room and her photographs will tattle in ways you aren't prepared to defend.

Bruce complains because she doesn't make him breakfast, doesn't clean the house, isn't everything he'd dreamed she'd be. He wouldn't feel that way, honestly, he says, if his mother had loved him, if she hadn't married that asshole after she left his father.

Em isn't going to tell her family, not for awhile. She feels ashamed. Bertrand is confused, sheepish, hangs back like a little boy as Em gathers the children together and waves good-bye. It's time to go, the horses need to be fed. No one notices really, it's all so abrupt, except the mother, who sees it in Em's slowed walk. The mother herself moves little these days, her feet swollen and infected. At night when she removes her shoes, unties the tight laces, she groans with the painful relief of it. The ulcers ooze as she soaks her feet each night, her husband in attendance. He doesn't dare recoil from the stench. Somehow he's given to understand this is his punishment for all he's made her suffer through the years, not the least of which was giving birth to fourteen children, two of whom died in infancy. He understands this is the deal. He knows too if it wasn't for her he'd have lost the farm long ago. She's somehow kept them on track, understood trends in the grain and livestock markets in ways others didn't. Her reputation in the valley of the Dead Horse Canyon is legendary and the old-timers still come to talk to her about her predictions. Perhaps she's a witch, a bit of the Druid in her, who knows. There won't be anything Em can keep from this mother, though. Nothing.

Perhaps the best thing for Bruce is a psychotic break, a complete breakdown now and then might do all of us good, Joanna thinks, a surrender to the exhaustion of keeping up pretenses, and goodness how he's had to pretend. There's nothing wrong with sinking into that meltdown of the mind. Drug therapy might offer a good change—something to make him happy. Bruce refuses it, though. Joanna's photographs continue to appear in newspapers everywhere. He can't seem to escape them no matter how far he travels. And people recognize him as the husband of . . . as though he's accomplished nothing on his own all these years. Of course he knows he's being petty and silly, jealous in the most infantile way. He's not a stupid man. It's the needy child in him, wanting all the attention, and only recently his therapist has pointed out that people who were neglected as children have an insatiable hunger to be loved. All he knows is he'd like to come downstairs to two eggs, hash browns, and toast each morning. Is that asking too much?

If his father could kill himself isn't he capable of the same thing? For a while it is a threat. How does Joanna resist such appeals? She has an album filled with photos from his successes, his graduation from medical school, promotions, award ceremonies. Is it possible she feels she has captured him, believes in the power of a photograph to steal a soul? He'll go nowhere until she's ready for him to leave? Maybe she's saying now, by saying nothing, she doesn't care what he does as long as he stops his interminable demands.

The mother had noted too, the day of the photograph, the secret smile on Alice's face. After years of living in a quiet house, so quiet that when she goes to visit this daughter she sinks into the quiet as one would into a feather bed, Alice is finally going to have a child. Her mother thinks back to that quiet house with its perfectly pressed doilies against the backs of chairs with arms still new. So much peace to give up. Alice doesn't know that yet. The mother says nothing of these things to her husband tonight. She has never talked to him. After he lifts her feet from the basin, he mentions what a tiring day it has been. She agrees a bit distractedly as he wraps the rough towel about her feet. He is very gentle. He was never gentle as a young man, always so rough and eager, so straight-on and impatient. Through the years he has become someone else, but still, she does not talk to him. Later, she will not talk to him about the death of Alice's only child, nor will she speak to him of Bertrand and Em and how tonight she can see their children, how they will grow up wild and untamed, uncared for. How they will never be satisfied, never really find love.

Bertrand claimed that after the second baby was born nothing was ever the same. It was a terrible birth, the doctor coming late and staying long into the night, a howling storm outside, the wind banging against the windows, and Bertrand having to help because there was no one else. He'd thought he could handle most anything having to do with birthing, being a rancher and all, but he'd never seen his wife in so much pain before. And there she was laid out on the kitchen table, trussed up like a turkey, her great belly heaving, blood and water, and a seeping goo, and screams he still can't forget. He'd never been able to see her the same again. And once the child was born, a daughter, he knew he'd not have the heart to try again. They slept in separate rooms after that, he moving a bed into the small upstairs room they had used to store odds and ends. It was cold up there, unlike the room he'd shared with Em.

"What's wrong with you that we can't ever have a decent looking place?" Bruce said that morning before she left for work. "What's wrong with wanting order? Who can blame a guy for wanting some order in his house?"

"Nothing's wrong with it," Joanna had said. "Wouldn't we all like to have someone take care of us." She gets home late after developing photos, making it always just under deadline, driving in the dark, through storms and everything else with some dippy reporter or another.

After their work is done, they're all keyed up and need to go out for drinks together. They're great friends despite the fact that they tend to antagonize each other the closer it gets to wrap. Ted doesn't really mind that she's called him an idiot only an hour ago, and she understands why Theresa has mocked her stress. She knows she should go home earlier given her husband's current preoccupations, his unhappiness, his goddamn breakdown, but she can't seem to muster the will to do the right thing. She's convinced that his version of the right thing is tweaked anyway. Another hour and she'll leave.

In the basement of their house Joanna has found an old leather satchel, something belonging to Bruce. Its weight tells her it is not empty. The satchel has not been hidden, only stored away all these years, unbothered as far as she can see, until now. She opens its clasps with a snap and there she finds his past life in photographs all piled loosely together, none in albums save a few gathered in a small red notebook. She sifts through them absently, picking up the occasional picture. But the red notebook she has saved for last. It is the photo journal of a trip, long ago, with a woman Bruce loved, a woman Joanna believes he still holds in his heart. Joanna feels a pang the instant she sees the first photo of Bruce and this woman together—they are kids really, the girl wearing her hair long and straight, parted down the middle, Bruce's hair shaggy and long, merging with his beard. There is pleasure in this ache, a strange hurt that fascinates her. She feels the need to twist a bit deeper and carefully turns the pages, lingering on some, like the one of the kiss. They've clearly set the timer and run together, dissolved into this kiss in which it appears they've lost track of the camera's eye, suddenly pulled into a passion they hadn't planned. She imagines the camera was left unattended for a while as they satisfied that quickening.

The truth is, this pain verifies what Joanna already knows: this isn't about breakfast. They never speak of the woman from the past. Perhaps that very silence is the alarm. The silent comparison that, though unspoken, rings against the walls. Joanna feels relieved by the reminder that she didn't have a chance. She looks through the camera's eyes into the eyes, much younger but still the same, of the man she has lived with for the past twenty-six years. She falls into those eyes that look so evenly into the camera's lens as though he has nothing to hide, a little taunting, see if you can really know me? But she, of all people, is adept at reading through the camera's lens and she does know him. All these many years later she finally does know him.

The mother had been a slender bride, standing there beside her groom who looked uncomfortable and not himself with his hair slicked back, before the priest. Only a small crowd. The wedding service seemed to go on and on. They'd both said their "I dos," and then gone to mingle with their friends and families, split up into gendered sides of the room, she with her sisters and her mother laying out food as though this wasn't a special day. She continued to work despite her sister's tutting, "It's only once you're married." And he, over there with his mates, being shoved and shoving back kidding each other out of their discomfort. She watched him, hoping to catch him glance her way, but he didn't, never once. Later, that night, it was clear neither of them had ever been touched, nor knew how to touch. They had not been patient with each other. Maybe it's the way of all first nights. And love? Well, is there love? Is that what's expected? Love seemed a luxury.

What was wanted was someone with a strong back and some life in her. The fact that she was slender had been a concern to her husband, maybe she wouldn't be strong enough to help him in the life he'd planned in America. They were leaving the very next day and he'd said she'd better be ready and she'd better not give him any trouble. He'd made this one promise to her, the scoundrel, she thought, "I'll give you anything I possibly can, anything money can buy as long as I have it," and clearly he was thinking of a brighter future than she, "but one thing you can't ever have is me. You understand, you'll never have me." She thought it strange, he's a strange one, she thought, but she was young and the night before had not been good. She felt a bit vague, a bit like she was underwater, her head pounding and her thoughts slightly muddled. What could she say? Nothing, which is exactly what she said. She thought he meant he wouldn't be faithful and the way she was feeling, that would be just all right with her. She would learn what he meant was much worse than that—she'd not have a claim on him. His intention was to remain independent, a man making his own decisions for himself. And so he did—for a while.

But here now, that man who said in such a boastful way she'd never have him, here's that same man drying her painful feet gently with a towel, as gently as her mother might have. He's the same man and not the same man. That's what she hadn't understood when she was young and slender. Maybe wisdom gave one girth. Maybe her broad mind, her wide experience are more than metaphor. She'll not share that with him either, her bit of humor. Besides, he's telling her now about the garden and how it's doing. She no longer tends such things, but he knows she's interested in the progress of the tomatoes, and the zucchini, and the beans. It's their agreement: he'll take care of the garden and she'll continue to make the bread. This is how simple, how lovely things have become. There are none of the old threats, the old boasts, none of the tantrums and manipulations of their youth. One could almost say such vanity has been burned out of them, left them older and more unwell, but sweeter too. Sweetened up for death, she thinks he'd say. And after the first night, they learned a few things about each other in the dark. She doesn't think in all their years together he's once betrayed her with another woman. She thought she had been prepared to accept anything, just as her mother and the church had taught her, but it turned out she hadn't been prepared at all.

Bertrand had been unreliable from the beginning. He's just stupid, you see, Em tells Merle. Merle is the only sister she can confide in, though she doesn't quite know why. Merle is the least experienced, and yet she seems tougher somehow. Em never feels she's shocking Merle. Merle listens quietly. "He's done it before, but I figured as long as he didn't flaunt it in my face, as long as he didn't involve the children, we'd just agree to not talk about it; I'd agree to not see what was right in front of my nose." She sniffles and swipes at that nose. Em crying, so out of character, Merle is tempted to surprise. She keeps her thoughts to herself. But Em misunderstands, thinks what she will about Merle's introspective look, her quiet, nonjudgmental ways, and goes on to talk about how Bertrand broke the unspoken rule. He was sloppy, let himself be seen with another woman, some floozie from Loup City. She and the children saw them together, swaying against each other giggling like a pair of teenagers. Em first glanced at the children—Bruce and Kathy—for their reaction, and their little mouths were hanging loose as they looked out the windows of the car. "Once a horse goes bad, there's nothing to be done for it." Em's not telling Merle this so she can get her advice; Em's not one for getting advice. She understands how she feels and exactly what she'll do with those feelings. No, she and the kids have already left that sorry ass excuse for a man. And he has the nerve, she tells Merle, to be surprised, to be contrite. Worse than any kid she's ever seen.

Joanna doesn't tell Bruce she's found the satchel of photographs. Neither does she tell him about the belt she found among them—a tooled leather belt with the name B-E-R-T-R-A-N-D pressed into the leather, rearing horses flanking the name. He never talks about his father.

She can't hope to explain to anyone else how now and then when she's feeling especially lonely she'll creep down the stairs with a load of laundry or some other errand and secretly look again at the face of her husband in the throes of love, a face she has never seen before. She can't explain even to herself how she cultivates that loneliness, how in her aloneness she sometimes feels more alive and more realized than when she is a part of something. Somehow she feels sure that even if Bruce happened upon similar photographs from her past he would not give them a second glance. He is not consumed as she is with trying to understand. It is not him she is trying to understand so much as something mysterious about life, something she can't seem to track but which she catches a trace of in those moments with his pictures, a likeness both familiar and altogether separate from herself.

A rupture has occurred in the blue room. One senses the rupture itself is not serious, though serious repercussions may be felt many years later. If things, as they now stand, come to an end in the lives of the occupants, the beginning of that end will be traced to this moment in the blue room. Small things at first, a treasured hurt, a relic to what has happened previous to this instant. Every misunderstanding, every ache and jelled resentment will find its source here. Betrayal—callousness—deceit—evil? None of those really, not from the message of the blue room, but rather the discovery that something necessary was never there. No, that's not it. In a moment of excitement, in a second of crisis, maybe nothing very important at all, someone made a choice which for someone else was wrong, and in that second is the end. But that can't be.

Beneath the smell of the dying leaves that comes through the closed windows is a slightly musty smell arising from the basement, from the old carpet, from the old furniture. The smell is negligible. One would have to be concentrating to notice it at all, but once it's been noted, it persists. The smell is neither pleasant nor unpleasant. Such smells simply define houses, a signature smell, some signatures more distinct than others.

Empty now, the blue room still seems inhabited, pulsing with an invisible breath. The quiet falls, palpable as snow, in the peace after the rush, a murmuring. Listening does not make the message clearer, but drives it into a feathery distance, as though attending it causes diffusion. It will simply dissipate like the wisp of a smell, the sound of a chord played, or a word spoken long ago.

Alan Lelchuk
Brooklyn Boy

Curt Leviant
Ladies and Gentlemen, The Original Music of the Hebrew
Alphabet *and* Weekend in Mustara: *Two Novellas*

David Milofsky
A Friend of Kissinger: A Novel

Lesléa Newman
A Letter to Harvey Milk: Short Stories

Ladette Randolph
This Is Not the Tropics: Stories

Sara Rath
The Star Lake Saloon and Housekeeping Cottages: A Novel

Mordecai Roshwald
Level 7

Lewis Weinstein
The Heretic: A Novel